To See Through Glass Darkly

by

C. R. Tranche

Published in 2009 by YouWriteOn.com

"Now we see through glass darkly,
then we shall see face to face."

Contents

Prologue

I am sitting in a small room, with one proper bed and one camp bed. The proper bed is for my mother and I sleep on the camp bed. There is a washbasin in the corner with a mirror where my mother spends a long time staring at herself. I don't know why because I am only four and this is one of my earliest memories. We buy food from a takeaway on the corner. This place is called a Bed and Breakfast but there is no Breakfast.

I am bored. I am staring out of the window and I can see three girls playing in the alley at the back of the hostel, laughing among the rattling cans and flapping newspapers with yesterday's stories of foreign wars.   One of them is in an old wheelchair. They look happy. The way they are clapping makes it look as though they must be singing. I love singing. I would like to sing with them. I wave shyly through the window; maybe the glass is too dirty, or they are too busy, but they don't wave back. I ask my mother if I can play with them and she says "With who?"

"With them," I reply, and point out of the window.

And she looks out of the window and says "There's nobody there."

I couldn't hear them. But I could see them.

That was the first time I remember seeing people who apparently didn't exist. It turned out that other kids who had stayed at that B&B reported seeing children in the alley and hearing them singing nursery rhymes. Someone said it must have been the ghosts of a refugee family who had stayed at the hostel for a long time and then been returned to their country and never been heard of again.

Now, I've never really written down these times when I have seen – what shall I call them – these "others". Partly that's because for a long time people thought I was weird enough anyway, without me adding to the impression. Partly, because I did not think other people would believe me, particularly as I was not even sure I believed myself sometimes. But mainly because there was not a lot to say. It was no big deal. No great story. Just sometimes, I would see or feel someone and then they would be gone. Like those children, or the man in the park in London who wore a strange peaked cap and uniform and who my teacher said sounded like an old fashioned park keeper. Or the shepherd walking up the hill behind the holiday cottage in Devon. Except there were no sheep and the grass he trod was mown only for golf.

So why write about it now? Because last night, those children from the B&B were in my dream. I've no idea why. They seemed to want something from me. Something I couldn't give them, but which they really needed. They were shouting up at me, but I was trapped behind that same murky glass, worlds apart. I woke up, sweating, feeling sick as if I had let everyone down and I fumbled my way to the bedroom window to get some air. I couldn't see anything except the shifting shadows of the trees, but I could hear them. Their sad songs and their cries echoed on the night wind and then, silence.

Chapter One: Signing Up

You know how you remember some dreams and forget others? Well, this one stayed with me, hung around in the back of my mind all the way to school on the bus as it bumped and lurched from our village into Canterton. I was still caught up in its web as I passed the huddle of smokers at the top gate and walked robotically down the drive, weaving my way in and out of the loitering students who were chatting, eating crisps, on their phones, sharing i-pods – anything to avoid actually going into school! It probably would have stuck around longer, if my Form Tutor, Mr Bettle, hadn't been distributing our Activity Week booklets at registration time. But that took precedence over everything!

It was called a week, but that wasn't strictly honest. In fact it was three days in June when all of Year 7 and 8 came off timetable and could choose between loads of different activities. As usual, some people were pretending that the whole idea was really boring and Toni made a great show of chucking her booklet in the bin saying she wasn't going to be seen dead on some kiddies' outings. But people in the year above had said it was good fun and if you think about it, anything has to be better than French and Geography and Maths! That week Year 9 had taster sessions for their GCSE options, Year 10 were on work experience and everyone else was taking exams. So I think the teachers were in for a pretty easy time.

My best friend Bridie and myself were flicking through the choices at break, sitting outside on the benches in the picnic area and stuffing doughnuts, which were the only edible things our canteen ever sold.

"If we keep eating like this we'll have to sign up to the Fun, Fit and Beautiful!" laughed Bridie.

"We'd never get a place. With Miss Gourly running it, there'll be a queue of at least two people," I joked, rather unfairly. I couldn't imagine anyone doing three days aerobics and make up with the frighteningly fierce and somewhat overweight ICT teacher whose idea of excitement was having a cup of tea in the computer server room whilst reading the most recent Microsoft Manual.

"What else is there?" chipped in Javaad, who had, as usual, got to school too late to make registration and had not picked up his copy. "By the way, do you realise this bench is meant to seat four? Budge up! You've eaten so many doughnuts you need your own reinforced seating arrangements for break."

We shoved up so we could all see the information.

"Here's something for you!" I said, very seriously. "Cooking!"

I wish I could have taken a picture of Javaad's face. His attempts in the Food Tech lessons had become a legend and it was only a matter of luck that neither Javaad, nor his family, nor anyone who had ever tasted his efforts had not died an early death from food poisoning.

"Using that logic," he replied "you should join the Art Class."

Fair point. But I like to think my work fits nicely into the modern art category – you know, great unidentifiable splodges of colour splashed all over the paper.

The three of us happily joked our way through the activities on offer. We had become friends pretty quickly when we all started at the beginning of Year 7 at Canterton Combined College. I had been terrified about moving up. My primary school had been a small homely place in my village, which is about 5 miles outside Canterton. But CCC had a reputation of being a tough, town comprehensive with loads of race problems and bullying. Well, that just shows

You shouldn't listen to gossip. It can be a bit scary – like when there was a big fight in the first term – and there are some people who bully (Toni, for instance) and others who mess about in all the lessons (unlike me, I only mess about in some of them) – but in the first six months I'd been there, I had really started to have fun. There is a buzz about my school, an edge to it, and that's good.

Making friends with Bridie and Javaad in my first few weeks had made all the difference. Admittedly we had our ups and downs during the first two terms. Some of the bombings and terrorist scares had caused a bit of tension with Javaad in particular, but we were never going to let prejudices like that really come between us. Javaad obviously spent quite a lot of time hanging out with some of the other Pakistani boys at school and I know they sometimes teased him about his friendship with Bridie and me, but that didn't stop him. Nothing much stops Javaad, he's very independent and determined when he gets going.

There were quite a few things in the activities booklet which interested me. I really like singing and the music teacher was running a three day songwriting and recording course. On the other hand, there was a chance to try riding and I have always secretly fancied myself as Showjumper of the Year, even though the nearest I have ever got to anything large with four legs was a giraffe at London zoo. I even have a photo of me and my birth mum standing in front of it when I was about four years old. The giraffe looks like some sort of crazy designer telescope, with long bendy legs; my mum looks beautiful from a distance and I don't know what I look like, because I've got my back to the camera!

It was the last time she took me anywhere and the only photo I have of her.

When I came to live here with my adoptive parents, when I was seven, I was so amazed that their house was almost in the country that I thought I could keep a horse in the back garden. I didn't realise you needed more than a lawn and a shed to keep a pony, but I have learned a lot since. Still, you have to start somewhere and I was privately convinced that once I sat on some prancing chestnut pony, my talents would all become clear! I read and re-read a book called "Straight to The Top!" where a girl found a foal and then broke it in. The next thing you knew was that her bedroom was practically wallpapered with rosettes and the organiser of the Junior British Team was on the phone, begging her to join them in Paris. In my dreams, that was going to be me! In reality, I thought that learning to ride with half of my year group watching me fall off whilst walking round a field on a leading rein was not going to do much from my self esteem, so I kept flicking through the booklet.

Now Bridie is a lot sportier than me so she was looking through the courses concentrating on things like trampolining and sailing. When most of us try to get out of PE by forgetting our kit or claiming injuries, Bridie is out there doing her stuff. Mind you, she is pretty good. She is on the county athletics squad and now they have the Olympics coming to London, I reckon she should be aiming high. Bridie's mum is quite plump (to put it kindly) and would always choose the sort of marathon you eat over the marathon you run, so I reckon Bridie must have inherited the superfast genes from her dad. I know he was a fast runner because Bridie always jokes that as soon as he knew her mum was pregnant, "he legged it so fast you'd think he was running the four minute mile!"

The problem was that we basically all wanted to spend activity week together, but you would no more get Bridie on a horse, than me on a trampoline or Javaad in a boat.

"What about this one?" said Javaad, looking right at the end of the booklet. "It's a three day residential at a place called Highwood House. You do all those ropes courses and wall climbing, but there's a lake as well so Bridie would be happy, and there's loads of other things you can choose – listen, night hikes, riding, football, windsurfing, recording studio, drama…"

"That would be perfect!" I cried, grabbing the page. "It's bound to be really popular. Let's get the parental permission slip signed tonight. It says it will be first come first served."

I am usually one of those girls whose letters home live their own mysterious lives, decomposing at the bottom of my school bag. Whenever my mum gets annoyed about it, I tell her I believe in recycling and that's just what the school letters are doing to themselves down there in the depths. They are composting, along with the uneaten cheese sandwiches. Somehow she doesn't find it funny. So she was quite surprised when I got home and went straight into the kitchen calling out:

"Mum! I'm home. I've got a letter from school!"

"Put it on the table and I'll look at it tomorrow," she called back. "I'm doing the early evening shift today and then I'm going on to meet your aunt for supper."

"Please Mum! Can't you just sign this before you go? It's really urgent!"

Mum came down in her white tunic and trousers. She's a physiotherapist and usually works during the day, but they have an evening session at the hospital which she does once a week. She always looks so professional and organised and although I've never seen her at work, other people have said she's really good. That makes me proud, even if she is a mother I acquired along the way, as it were.

She checked her watch.

"This is a turn up for the books, you usually say letters from school are a waste of the world's trees."

"This one's about Activity week," I explained and went on to tell her about the residential. I knew she would be pleased. I always used to be considered shy. On top of that, I have eavesdropped on enough conversations to know that adopted kids are "often trouble when they are teenagers". So the fact that I appear to have settled in to CCC without too much grief and have made friends has made her and Dad very happy.

"Well, skimming through it, I must say it looks like a great idea. It is quite a bit of money, though, but I expect your dad won't mind. Chris is going to France, so I suppose it's only fair. I have worked with some disabled children who have been riding at Highwood and it sounds a really well run place."

"What sort of disabled?" I asked.

Mum replied as she fished around in the kitchen drawer for a pen that worked. "All sorts. It's amazing to see kids in wheelchairs sort of set free by getting the freedom of riding."

That was what they had wanted last night, I thought to myself, the children in the dream: they wanted to be set free. I don't think mum noticed me shiver as she signed the piece of paper and before I knew it, she had left, revving out of the drive like a formula one driver because she was late!

Chris' permission slip was on the table as well. I think the only reason he has signed up for the French Trip at his grammar school was to try to smuggle home cheap cigarettes. He's three years older than me and when I went into his room the other day to nick his memory stick, the whole place stank of smoke and his bedroom window was open. I told him that all girls think that boys who smoke are gross and that no-one is ever going to kiss him if he reeks like an ashtray, but he told me to take my enormous nose out of his business. (This is mean, because he knows I have a thing about the size of my nose.) He said it was his choice if he wanted to die of lung cancer and I told him it wasn't because it would cost the health service a huge amount of money and we started arguing. Again.

If you haven't guessed by now, Chris is my older brother. Not my real brother. To be fair, it can't have been easy for him having some adopted little sister turn up when he was seven, just when he must have thought the world would continue revolving around him for ever. I'm not sure I would have been as kind as he has, if I had been in his shoes and although we do bicker, I count that as a sign of a pretty normal relationship.

I made the effort to put my form straight back inside my planner. "Getting everything ready the night before" never has been one of my strong points, but this was going to be an exception.

The next day at school, Javaad even made it to registration brandishing his signed parental permission slip triumphantly. Two of his friends, Lewis and Salim were going to sign up too. I liked Lewis, but Salim was trouble. Funny, good looking – but trouble. But as soon as Bridie came into our form room I could see there was a problem. We weren't allowed to wear make up to school, and I never bothered, but Bridie usually wore a bit of eye shadow and mascara and today it was smudged under her red eyes. She had been crying. We headed off to the toilets, telling Javaad to let Mr Bettle know where we were so we weren't marked in late and got yet another 10 minute after school detention.

"What's the problem?" I asked, as Bridie washed her face and scrabbled in her pencil case to find her mascara to repair the damage. I leaned against the washbasins, close to the windows, mainly to avoid the disgusting smell of school toilets and disinfectant. When we were looking round secondary schools in Year 6, I remember hearing one of the mothers at my village primary school talking to another. She was saying that when she went to open evenings, she didn't take much notice of the Headteacher's talk, or the displays on the wall, or the number of computers. She used to sneak away and check out the students' toilets. "And that," she had finished "is the reason why no child of mine will ever go to that dreadful Canterton Combined College."

Looking around, I could see that the graffiti in three different languages and the broken loo door could give a bad impression. Certainly for the first term, I would suffer agony rather than risk being brave enough to go into the loos and fight my way through the gossiping Year 10 girls. But now, these toilets were a familiar stopping off point between Maths and French for a chat, or when you needed to quietly disappear – like now…

"I can't go on the residential," said Bridie.

"Why not?" I asked, but then stopped myself almost before I had finished speaking. Of course, the money. When the packing factory had closed down earlier in the year, a lot of people had lost their jobs in Canterton. Bridie's mum was a childminder and most of the kids she looked after had mums working at the factory. Her dad never sent anything, so cash had been pretty tight for them recently. If Bridie couldn't go, I wouldn't go either. It was as simple as that.

"We had a big row about it this morning," said Bridie. "I feel so bad. I know mum does her best, but I really wanted to go. I just slammed the door and left and she was crying. It was so unfair of me."

Bridie started crying again and I hugged her, not really knowing what to say. I had been part of a very poor set up when I was small, in those Bed and Breakfast days and occasionally blurred memories of the empty fridge and no milk returned to me. But it all seemed a long time ago now and I felt guilty that I had so much at the moment, and she had so little. Life wasn't fair. Suddenly, I remembered something. Maybe those school letters weren't such a waste of trees after all.

"Bridie, stop! Listen! I've got an idea."

"What?"

"That letter which went with the form and the activity booklet. It said that if there were any problems with money, then parents should contact Mrs Allan and there may be funds available to help."

Bridie sniffed and took out her mascara. "Mum would never phone the Head," she said, peering into the smeared mirror. "She's too proud."

"Well, there's no harm in us just talking to Mrs Allan about it," I persisted. "Come on, it's worth a try. If there's money around, I'd much rather you got it than some slimeball like Toni who grabs everything that's going."

I'll tell you more about Toni later, but if I start now, I'll never stop. There probably aren't enough pages in all the books in the world to describe someone as mean as her.

Anyway, at breaktime, we made our way up to the top corridor where the teachers live. And I mean live. I seriously wonder if some of them ever go out at all. You see them scuttling in through the swing doors marked "No entry for students", dragging their shopping bags of marking and then that's it. They disappear into some alternative dark universe of reports, detention letters and cups of tea. Overcome with giggles, we had to face the wall whilst Mr Gannick limped past, wafting his damp armpits past us as he passed through the doors.

"Go on, knock!"

"No, you knock, this is your idea."

"Your money!"

Then we both knocked together and it sounded really loud and we started giggling again.

Luckily Ms Midler answered. She is a young PE teacher and really nice. We think she has something going on with the student teacher in the Department but no-one actually has any evidence. It would be nice if it was true, however. Romantic!

"What on earth is up with you two?" she laughed.

"We wondered if we could see Mrs Allan" I asked. "It's really important and won't take long."

Miss Midler opened the door. "Well, she's very busy, but I did just see her in the staffroom. Wait there and I'll see what I can do."

A couple of minutes later and the Head came out. She knows us because she teaches us RE once a week. Needless to say, we all try really hard in her lessons, hand the homework in on time, put our hands up and answer questions, bring the text book every week. Even Salim makes a passable effort at doing some work.

"Hello Ellie, morning Bridie! How can I help?" she smiled. She was quite a smiley person considering she was a Headteacher.

Bridie looked at me. That's what comes of not being the shy one any longer.

"It's about Activity Week," I started.

Ms Allan interrupted me immediately. "Hang on right there! You should know I do not, repeat not, have any influence at all on who gets what. That's totally up to Miss Nicolson and I wouldn't dare interfere!" We all laughed. It was funny to think that even the Headteacher was scared of the hyper-efficient Miss Nicolson who patrolled the Languages Department with a clipboard and a briefcase and was in charge of allocating places for Activity Week.

"No, it's not that." I said. "It's just that Bridie really wants to come on the residential with us, but since the packing factory closed, her mum hasn't got many kids any longer." I could see Mrs Allan was looking puzzled.

"She doesn't mean her own kids," Bridie explained. "Mum's a childminder and most of the babies' and toddlers' mums worked at Packers. They've lost their jobs so they don't need a childminder any longer."

I took up the story again. "So that means it's really hard for them to pay for the residential, because Bridie's dad doesn't send any money. She gets free school meals, if you need proof." I stopped, a bit embarrassed and caught Bridie's eye. Had I said too much? But we know each other so well now that Bridie could read my expression and she carried on.

"I know the letter says mum should contact you, but she won't because she's too proud."

Mrs Allan thought for a moment.

"Leave it with me to think about it," she said. And that was that. I would like to be that sort of person. Wise and thoughtful. Instead I usually charge into things and blab my great mouth off and then regret it for weeks, months –life even!

Later that night, on line, Bridie and I were talking. I could tell Bridie was totally over excited by the gobbly gook she was typing.

"MrsA called my mum. Aaahhh. I thought mumwouldbefuriousbutitsallok. **IMGOING ON THE RESDNTAL YYYEEE AAAHHH**

(Yes! Just like that. She always misses the space bar when she gets over excited and can't spell very well at the best of times!)

It turns out that the Head had rung really tactfully and discussed the whole thing with Bridie's mum and they only had to pay half.

The letter confirming our places arrived about a week later. After half term, we would be going to Highwood on the residential trip. Their slogan was "Experience a Different World!" And as I lay in bed that night, imagining what the trip would be like, the slogan reminded me of my dream, that other world, and when I slept those children came back again, asking me for something which I couldn't provide.

Chapter Two: The Big Break

More letters, more forms, more dead trees – all to get ready for the Highwood residential. Firstly, the health forms. No problem there. Physically, I am disgustingly healthy. I have had my illnesses in the past, but there again, life wasn't always as easy for me as it is now. When I was younger and in care, I didn't eat much or speak much. As a result (and not surprisingly) I was thin and silent! As you have probably gathered, I have been making up for that period of my life recently by eating and talking for England.

Then you had to put "religion". I left it blank. My Mum and Dad go to church every now and again, so I suppose I am theoretically Church of England. I go with them sometimes and that, combined with those "others" I told you about, I do have this feeling that there may be something else out there. Chris brought home some Shakespeare homework one evening and one of the lines was highlighted. Now, don't get me wrong, I am not some sort of child genius who read Macbeth when I was six years old, but for some reason this line jumped off the page at me:

"There are more things in heaven and earth than our dreamed of in our philosophy"

Or something like that. I may have misquoted it. But basically it means that us human beings may think we know everything with our science and maths and technology, but out there – like when you stare up at the black sky and study the stars or listen to the sea on a stormy day – there are things we haven't even begun to understand.

Back to the real world and those forms. Basically – no, I have no special dietary requirements – I am a human dustbin. I eat anything and everything and especially chocolate, expensive ice cream and grapes! Bridie goes through phases of being a vegetarian, but it usually collapses as soon as anyone produces a hot dog.

The next form is the insurance one. I didn't consider spending three days in a Youth Activity centre a particularly dangerous thing to do. What sort of dangers could you possibly face on a Year 7 Adventure week?

Finally, there was THE LIST. IE What to take. Here is what my list looked like by the time I had finished studying it at the kitchen table, with Bridie ringing up every two minutes with helpful, or more accurately, not so helpful, suggestions.

Towel (1 for 4 days, including swimming? No way!)

Washbag (OK for me, but for Bridie this is going to have be a wash holdall)

Pyjamas (No! I cannot possibly take the ones with pink elephants. URGENT! Buy new pyjamas!)

Old Clothes - Remember! You will be getting very muddy on the outdoor activities.

(Not helpful advice. All my old clothes are just that – old and disgusting which is why I don't want to be seen dead or alive in them.)

Wellington Boots

Trainers

Smart clothes for the end of stay Disco. (Massive panic.)

Swimming costume (My bikini creeps up my bottom.)

Swimming Hat (Never. Not even on pain of execution.)

Anorak (Who are these people? Birdwatchers from the 70s?

Riding Hat – If you have one (I don't, but wish I did.)

Spare Underwear

Sleeping Bag

Pillow case

Please note: NO MOBILE PHONES, I-PODS or VALUABLES

So I have added:
Mobile Phone
I-Pod
Money
And later:
Frog (Green, squashed and a bit smelly, but I have not slept without him - ever!)
Hairdryer
Hat (I like hats)

I have also written "things?" which is a sort of secret reference to the fact that I have not started my periods and am terrified it may all happen when I am not at home. Nightmare.

Then there was the parent meeting at school for people going to Highwood. My Mum sat with Bridie's mum and we sat in front, putting a respectable distance between us and them. Javaad's parents never really showed up to school stuff, but times like this, when someone had to come, one of his brothers or uncles came instead. This time it was Numan, and he stood at the back with Javaad, looking cool, gorgeous and bored. Mrs Seddon, our Head of Year, showed a DVD of the centre which looked pretty impressive, based around a huge six hundred year old house!

"Is it haunted, Ms Seddon?" yelled Salim.

Since he hadn't put his hand up, he was ignored by the icy Head of Year, although a few parents chuckled. I didn't. I couldn't see how a house like that could have witnessed that much history and not be home for some of its restless spirits from the past. The parents' questions were a lot more tedious than Salim's.

"They're forecasting a heatwave. What would happen then?" What do you think would happen? It would get hot, we would all spend our time sunbathing in an attempt to go

brown. Well, those of us who weren't brown already, anyway!

"Would the children have access to plenty of water?" What? We are not going to the Sahara desert!

"Are the coaches safe?" If I had been Ms Seddon, I would have said "No! We have deliberately searched the country looking for the most unsafe coaches we can find so everyone can suffer horribly in a crash on the motorway."

How she kept her cool, I've no idea. On and on they went, these parents who feel they just have to say something at every meeting. Even my mum was starting to fidget and whisper to Bridie's mum.

"Behave yourself you two," I joked, turning round and wagging my finger at them. They laughed. My minded started drifting away as I stared at the stage in the school hall.

Very soon, that was going to be me standing up there. Me, with Shareen, Liam and Adrian singing in the first round of the Battle of the Bands. Terrifying!

Let me explain. If you haven't heard of it, Battle of the Bands is a competition for any band or group, aged between 11 – 16. Firstly, you have to win nomination by your school – and each school can have two bands in the competition – and then you go through to the regional final, with bands from ten other secondary schools in the area. The prize for winning at that level is a session in a recording studio and you go on to a national final in London, with top judges from "the industry". Even if you only come second in the regional finals you win some huge amount of money to spend on music and instruments and things like that.

Sometimes at night, in my room, when Mum and Dad think I am doing my homework, I download a song, grab my pencil case and stomp up and down on my bed imagining we are on stage in the finals. Alright, I admit. This whole thing has gone slightly to my head ever since Shareen asked me if I would sing with her in a band.

It was after Karaoke Club at lunchtime. Shareen and I have been singing together for a while, even though she is in Year 8. She has a stronger voice than me: it's really rich, sexy and bluesy. She's from Ghana originally, in Africa, and when you think about it, lots of the really good singers are black African. I don't so much sing with her, but in more of a backing role. My voice and hers go well together. I can reach some of the higher notes and, although I say it myself, I'm pretty good at holding a harmony.

I knew that Shareen and a couple of her Year 9 friends had been chatting about getting a band together and entering the competition because I'd heard them in the music rooms, planning, whilst Liam jammed on his guitar and Adrian took out all the Year 9 exam stress on the drum kit. I had been thinking to myself "that'll be me in a couple of years" when Shareen caught up with me in the canteen and sat down.

"You know Liam, Adrian and me are getting a group together for the Battle of the Bands," she started.

I nodded, mouth full of pasta.

"Well, I wondered if you would like to sing with us. With our band. Don't get your hopes up, we'll probably be rubbish, but it would be fun. What do you think?"

I nodded, wildly this time, mouth still full of pasta.

"Of course, if you don't want to, don't worry…it's not a big deal or anything," Shareen said, pushing back her chair.

"Stop! Don't be ridiculous! Of course I want to!" I shouted. Then of course I realised that half the school were looking at me and I felt really embarrassed. People picked up their knives and forks and trays and the noise and chatter started up again, breaking the silence.

"If you're going to be that embarrassing, I'm not sure we want you!" laughed Shareen. But she went on "Look, that's great. We have to do two numbers and we've got to be ready in four weeks time, so we're going to have to do some rehearsing. Adrian's going to play drums, Liam on guitar and a bit of vocals, and you and me singing. We think it would be a lot better if we had someone on keyboard – any ideas? We are a bit short on instrumentalists and Nicki and Toni's band is going to be amazing."

"I'll think about it," I said, "see who I can think of." Anything to beat Toni.

"Great. See you in the music room after school. We've booked a room. We should be finished at about 5. Is that OK?"

"Brilliant," I said.

Absolutely, unbelievably brilliant.

I told mum I wouldn't be coming home on the school bus. Luckily, in the summer term she doesn't have such a fit about me walking into town and meeting her after work, so there was no big hassle about lifts.

By the end of the day I was so excited, and nervous, I couldn't concentrate at all. Double ICT at the end of the day was the last straw. Sitting up in the computer rooms making a vague attempt to get my Excel spreadsheet to behave itself whilst Ms Gourly rampaged up and down the desks trying to catch people on the internet before they pressed minimize; staring out of the window at the hot blue sky and the mothers with their little kids walking home from nursery with their sun hats on; putting the head phones on and secretly listening to music and thinking one day that will be our band.......all this just waiting, waiting for the bell.

"Ow!"

Javaad had just kicked me hard.

"What did you do that for?" I asked angrily, at the top of my voice, forgetting how loud your voice sounds when you are listening to music with headphones on.

Javaad was making weird facial expressions and jerking in a very odd way. Then I noticed Ms Gourly, standing staring at me. Ah. Now I know why he kicked me!

"Ellie, I am very disappointed. You know very well that you are not allowed to listen to music from the internet during ICT lessons. Close that down immediately and take those headphones right off."

She swung round to address the rest of the class, hands on her spreading hips, shrieking slightly in an attempt to be heard above the noise of people chatting, packing up and scraping their chairs. "Stop it! I have not asked you to pack up yet! I am waiting!"

They always say that, don't they? It's usually quite obvious that they are waiting and that we don't care. But I suppose as a rather limited strategy, it does work. So we all sat down reluctantly, and looked at her bulging eyes and throbbing face. Off she went again.

"Those of you who have not managed to complete your spreadsheets because you have been wasting your time will stay behind for 15 minute to catch up. Ellie, that includes you, as well as Toni, Louise, Ibrar and Lee. The rest of you may pack up."

I couldn't believe it. The whole day had gone so slowly and now I had to do another fifteen minutes. Shareen might think I had just not bothered to turn up. Putting on my sweetest smile and trying to hide the fact that I was still wearing my trainers from lunchtime, I sidled up to her desk.

"Excuse me, Ms Gourly. I am sorry about this lesson, but I was wondering if I could possibly do the 15 minutes another time, like tomorrow lunchtime, as I am meant to be at a rehearsal in the music room after school."

"You should have thought of that before," snapped Ms Gourly predictably. "Sit down. Oh and whilst I have you here, why are you wearing trainers instead of regulation school shoes?"

It was going to be a long fifteen minutes. I tried to get a message to Bridie to ask her to tell Shareen what was going on. But the computer witch had forbidden all communication and Bridie was desperate not to miss athletics training. The clock crawled round and the pointless Excel spreadsheet, recording the number of cans of pet food needed at a fictitious kennel still refused to behave. The dogs all ended up in the pet food column and the computer seemed to have concluded that I would need a total of 312,587 cans of food to feed five dogs for a month. Which can't be right, unless they were monstrous dinosaur dogs from hell. I was released from prison at 3.45 on the dot and I charged from the ICT room, down the stairs, under the covered walkway, across the grass (forbidden) and into the new music school in record time.

"So sorry...." I gasped, almost unconscious with exhaustion as I fell though the doors. "Ooops! Wrong rehearsal room!" I stuttered to the rows of the chamber choir chanting Latin hymns.

"So sorry..." I gasped again, this time to the right people in the right room.

"No problem!" laughed Adrian. "Javaad came over and told us that the Gourly Witch had captured you!"

Javaad was kind like that.

"We thought we should try to do two different numbers in the competition" said Shareen. "One well known and one of our own. Liam is a great songwriter and he's got a couple of ideas."

"We thought a track by that mate of yours, Rick James," chipped in Adrian, "I'll Come Running" or one of those."

Adrian was exaggerating a bit by referring to the number one rock star as my mate, but it was now known all over town that he had been a real friend to me ever since he had played at the festival the Youth Council organised earlier in the summer. I'd known him when I was small. He was a teacher at my special school in London and he'd kept a promise he'd made to me then, that he'd always help me if he could.

"That would be good," I replied. If it's any help, I expect he'd send us the music if we get a keyboard player."

"Liam and Shareen were about to let us hear this song they've been working on together," said Adrian, fingers still tapping. That's the thing about drummers. They are always tapping – in the canteen, in lessons, on the school bus. Tap, tap, tap.

Liam and Shareen started. It was sad song, which got right under my skin. The lyrics were all about moving away and saying goodbye, which might sound pretty clichéd, but actually they were really original. That and the melody, which kept coming back in a chorus. I picked it up second time round and came in with a bit of harmony, and Adrian picked up the drum sticks. It sounded fantastic.

"Watch out London, here we come!" joked Shareen and each of us dreamed our own dream about winning the first round of the competition. Standing on the school stage in the glare of the lights, the judges on their feet, applauding us and the crowd going wild..........

"Ellie, I don't think you've been listening to a thing!" I heard my Mum saying.

And there I was, in the school hall – yes – but at the Highwood House parents evening! It had finished, apparently, and I had been miles away! There was so much to look forward to this second half of term that my head was buzzing with a sick making mixture of apprehension, fear and excitement: round one of the Battle of the Bands, Highwood

House Activity Week, the regional finals...if only we could get through.

Chapter Three: The New Member of the Band

There may have been loads of exciting things coming up in the future, but that did not mean that life was not pretty boring in the meantime. Take weekends, for instance.

Now, I know some people go shopping, but to be honest, I have never been that big on shopping. Bridie, Rachel, Hayley – they can all shop 'till they drop' as the saying goes, but me? My legs start to go wobbly and I get an overwhelming urge to spend hours sitting in cafes drinking hot chocolate. Then there's sport. Bridie goes training on Sunday afternoons, so that rules her out. Javaad plays football Sunday mornings with a local team. Even Hayley goes swimming with her sister. Which leaves me feeling like a bit of a pie at home. My dad has the solution. It's called "going for a walk". He thinks it's one of the big plus points about living just outside town.

"We can just step outside the front door and in a few minutes we're in beautiful walking country," he says to visitors.

Which I interpret as "We can just step outside the front door and straight into a cowpat."

In fact, if you turn left out of our front door, you go past our neighbours who have an old police dog who barks like crazy, up the lane to the main road where my school bus picks us up and drops us off. If you turn right, you go straight onto a footpath and this was the way we set off on a compulsory jolly family Sunday walk through the woods. They're called the Bluebell Woods for a reason. At this time of year, I have to admit they are amazing. The whole floor of the forest is bright blue, shimmering in the breeze like the sea on a summer's day.

If there is a heaven, I think it must be something like those woods which are sweet and peaceful, with the sun flickering through the solemn beech trees and the paths soft and kind under your feet.

Mum and dad always walked faster than me and they were some way ahead, when I heard the laughing. I looked back. The footpath was deserted. Something flickered at the edge of my sight, rustling the bluebells and shaking the low hanging branches. Someone running? Playing hide and seek? I felt the familiar tightness in my throat, my dry mouth. We were not alone in the forest, but the company was not malicious or evil. No, it felt young, playful. I reached the stile and turned round. There! Running straight into the low dazzling sunlight, silhouettes of children, waving and then gone. Maybe this place was like heaven in more ways than I had thought.

"What are you waiting for Ellie?" called mum, some way ahead.

I wish I knew the answer to that, I thought. But I called out loud, "Nothing! I'm coming!" I speeded up, wondering why it was children who seemed to be my uninvited company at the moment, in my dreams, in these woods. What did they want from me?

Anyway, there was no way they would accompany me on the other side of the woods, beyond the stile. The footpath crossed a barren field, heading towards a farm, and we stumbled scratching our legs on thistles and avoiding the nettles. Dark clouds which had started to build up in the distance slid across the sun and quite suddenly it felt colder, darker.

"Do we have to go this way, dad?" I asked. "I hate going through the farmyard."

"It's a very long way if we go all the way round," he called back. "And all three of us need to get back to do some work before tea."

Despite being a London girl by birth, I didn't hate farmyards in general. When we had been on holiday in Devon we had walked through quite a few, with hens and tractors and even with barking sheepdogs, but that had been fine. It was just this farm that made me wary. As we got closer, the field became littered with old machinery. The rusting prongs of a broken plough looked like skeletons' fingers clawing their way out of the dry earth and pushing their way up through the yellowing grass, coils of barbed wire reached out and grasped your legs and cans and plastic drums lay on their side, leaking foul fluids over the soil. It was as if we had walked from heaven into hell.

All three of us paused, silently and apprehensively, to check that the farm dogs were safely chained up, and I felt a mixture of sadness and fear when I walked quickly past them. They looked so angry, straining against their chains and baring their teeth. The rising wind knocked a piece of old iron against a barn door and two calves, knee deep in manure, stood miserably side by side. But that was nothing compared to what we saw beyond the barn. Two ponies were tethered to a metal post in a small, bare paddock. Their heads were hanging low and every now and again they stamped their hooves in the dust and a swarm of flies rose up and then settled back down on their eyes, as if they were already dead.

"Dad, that's awful! You must go and knock on the door. No-one should be allowed to keep ponies like that," I cried.

Mum paused and looked at the ponies. "Ellie's right" she said. "They don't seem to have any water and it's quite a hot day."

"It's not just that!" I said. "Look, their halters are digging into their necks, and they've no grass at all and look at the flies….."

"Ellie, calm down!" said dad, quite sharply. "We'll talk about this later." He opened the gate and set off along the lane towards home. I could see why. Mr Wilton, the farmer, was standing at the door of an old shed, staring at us angrily. He didn't look too friendly and despite my tendency to rush in without thinking, even I thought it might be better to plan a campaign rather than take him on, there and then.

But when we got home, dad didn't seem to want to spend much time discussing the ponies. He went off up to his study to catch up on some work. He works for the NHS, something to do with organising the people who work in the hospital.

"Its all very well you spending all your life looking after people" I yelled up the stairs. "What about the animals? Someone's got to speak up for them!"

"Ellie, your dad's busy. He's got a lot on his plate this week," said Mum. "Come and sit in the kitchen. I'm putting the kettle on and we can think about what to do."

We talked it through, Mum and I. Personally I couldn't see what there was to think about or talk about. It was quite obvious. We had to ring the Animal Rescue people and ring them fast. The ponies might not live much longer and the farmer was obviously a cruel and horrible man. Mum didn't see it that way. She thought we should walk that way again next weekend and see if the ponies were still there. If they were, and if they still looked poorly kept, then we could ring.

"They may not be that badly looked after," she said. "They may have been in that paddock just for the afternoon. Or sometimes, ponies have to be kept away from the rich summer grass because it makes them ill. We mustn't jump to conclusions."

"Oh, and I suppose they have to be kept away from water and shelter as well, in case that makes them ill," I left the sarcasm ringing round the kitchen and stamped upstairs to my

36

room. I know that was rude, but sometimes, when things are really important, I feel I have to be rude just be heard.

I logged onto my computer and googled "horse rescue". Lots of sites came up, including places which take in and look after mistreated ponies, the RSPCA and various news stories about horses which had been found in horrible conditions and been rescued by concerned members of the public. IE people like me and NOT like Mum, Dad and Chris. Still, I knew only too well some official from a charity would probably want to speak to an adult and I would get nowhere on my own if I rang up. I would have to follow mum's plan and see how they were next weekend. And that would be after the Battle of the Bands first round and just before going to Highwood House. Which seemed a long way away, both for me and the ponies.

I switched to my inbox and picked up my e-mails before shutting down. There were three: one from High Miss, a clothes shop who had somehow put me on their mailing list because I once bought a hideous skirt from them on line – apparently, I had been selected to have a £10 voucher next time I shopped on line with them. "Yes, me and one million other people who made the mistake of buying your ugly clothes," I thought crossly. The second e-mail was from Rachel, sending me some photos of her birthday party which were hilarious and where I appeared to look like a raving lunatic with a deformed face. The last one was from Shareen and it read,

"Good news. I've found a keyboard player! Rehearse at Adrian's house tomorrow at 6pm? Final lyrics attached. See ya. xx Shareen"

Why didn't she say who the new member of the band was? I opened up the attachment with the lyrics and while it was printing off, I texted her.

"Who is it?"

"waitnsee!" she replied.

So, I was still in a state of total ignorance when I turned up for rehearsal on Monday after school and banged on Adrian's garage door. I could hear Adrian drumming away. He obviously couldn't hear me, so I pushed my way in and helped myself to a Coke and Brownie which Adrian's dad had kindly left for us just as he was leaving for work. We had just started to speculate about the mystery keyboard player, when the door banged again and in came, in came.....well, in came Shareen with George Webber.

Now, that won't mean much to you right now, but believe me, of all the 1200 people who go to Canterton Combined College, the last person I ever expected to see walk into Adrian's garage was George Webber. Four days to go until the Battle of the Bands and Shareen walks in with George Webber, carrying a keyboard.

Adrian's face was hilarious. He had actually stopped tapping, that's how bad it was. And Liam, who was following Shareen, looked a bit green. I have no idea what my expression was, but I know I was thinking inside my head that there was a mistake. George must have been passing and Shareen must have asked him to carry the keyboard for her and then he was going to leave and someone else – someone like Ross Manning in Year 10 or some cool dancer like Gabriel Side – someone else would come in and say "Hi! I'm the new member of the band."

But no, there was no mistake. George Webber, weird, podgy and so, so posh George Webber from my year group was our new keyboard player.

The rest of us had changed after school, so George standing in a garage in his school trousers (slightly too short) and his school sweatshirt (much too big) and his glasses looked totally out of place. But typically, he didn't even seem to notice. That was what was so odd about George. He was seriously brainy and put his hand up in lessons to answer all the questions, apparently not even vaguely aware of the fact that everyone giggled. He sat and ate on his own in the canteen without even looking as though he felt self-conscious. He spoke like Prince Charles and looked curious when kids imitated him; he wore corduroy trousers and woolly jumpers on non-uniform day; he gave his English talk on violas and he read Wuthering Heights during wet breaks.......I could go on.

There were also things he didn't do. He didn't swear, for instance. He never had people round to his house. He didn't play football (although apparently he is quite good at rugby). He was just one of life's different people. Not one I intended to hang out with, for fear of committing social suicide, but not one I hated either. And not one I intended to sing alongside on stage in the Battle of the Bands, if I had any choice in the matter. But it didn't look as though I did have any choice. George got right down to work.

"If I use this socket, will it overload the power supply?" he said, peering at the lead from the keyboard and an extension plug which went to the amps and Liam's electric guitar.

No hi, or I'm George or anything like that.

"Do you want a coke?" asked Shareen.

"Your dad knocked the dustbin over with his bike," said Liam.

All almost at the same time. The whole thing was getting more bizarre, more random by the minute and I got the giggles.

"No, I don't think so," said Adrian (referring, I think, to the power supply).

"No, I tend to avoid things like that," said George (referring, I think, to the coke)

"No, I picked it up," said Shareen (referring, I think, to the dustbin).

Silence.

"Shall we start again?" I asked between giggles and everyone else laughed. Well, George didn't exactly laugh, but he did smile and Shareen grinned as well.

"Yeah! Good idea, Ellie! This is George. I guess you know him. He's in your year group isn't he? I was chatting to Ms Hensome about us needing a keyboard player and she said they don't come any better than George. So I asked him, he said yes, and here we are!"

Shareen had this knack of always being incredibly smiley and positive about everything.

"Uh..Great!" I managed to say, partly to distract attention away from Adrian who was glaring at Shareen and making faces. I could see that he was thinking that George wasn't exactly going to make a positive contribution to our image. "Let's get going then".

So we set up the keyboard, sat George on an upturned recycling box and got everything switched on and tuned up. I gave George the music to "On my Way" and we played. And we played like we'd never played before. Whatever else you could say about George, one thing was true: he was an unbelievable musician. His improvisation just lifted our whole act from sounding like a reasonable karaoke job to a real live performance. And something strange seemed to happen to George when he played. He came alive. Not in a particularly cool way, but his whole face and body relaxed and his fingers flew up and down the keys as if he had been born to make music.

When the last few bars were finished, we all just stopped and stared and then turned to George, and without planning, we gave him a great big round of applause! He nodded. Liam lifted his hand to high five him, but George just sort of looked up and Liam ended up clouting him over the head instead by mistake. When we had all finally recovered from hysterics, we got down to business.

"So, all we need now is a name," said Liam.

"And fast!" added Adrian. "They need it by tomorrow evening so the programmes will be printed in time."

Well, we went through everything you can think of. Liam came up with dreadful stuff like the Warriors (because of the Battle of the Bands.....how bad is that?) and The Armour Plated Act which was plain ridiculous. Adrian's contributions were less odd but equally dreadful.

"What about the Garage Group?" he suggested.

"But we don't even play garage, quite apart from the fact that it's a dreadful name," complained Shareen.

I was thinking about our names and wondering if the initials would spell anything. Shareen, Liam, Adrian and now, George (I'd forgotten myself.)

"S, L, A, G, " said Liam, thinking out loud – and then of course, we all cracked up. "SLAG! Not quite the image we're looking for!"

"We could suggest Nicki and her vile little sister Toni use it for their band!" joked Liam. I admit we all laughed – it may have been rude, but it would be a very appropriate name for their group.

When we were finally able to talk again, Shareen said "Not SLAG maybe, but how about GLAS – or glass. I don't know, Breaking Glass. Or Glass something."

We all tried it out. It seemed to grow on us.

"Glass Darkly," said George.

"Glass what?" we chorused.

"Glass Darkly," repeated George. "It's a saying from the Bible. Now we see through a glass darkly, but then we will see clearly. I suppose it means that life can seem really weird and confusing, but that one day it will all make sense."

"And it's about growing up, isn't it?" added Shareen. "About putting aside childish things?"

Liam looked at her as if she had suddenly metamorphosed into a professor of theology!

Shareen caught sight of his expression. "I bet you didn't know that I go to church. With my mum. That's where I started singing."

I had been thinking. "It also sounds like its talking about other worlds, doesn't it? Oh, shut up Adrian!" I laughed. "You know what I mean. Sort of ..." I struggled for the word, "sort of spiritual. How we humans always think we know everything about everything, but I bet we don't."

I was thinking about the strange bottle I had found the year before which had allowed me to capture the spirit of places; I was also remembering those "others" who criss crossed my path through life. Most vividly, I was seeing in my mind's eye, the refugee girl in the wheelchair and hearing in my mind's ear the laughter of the children in the forest. But I wasn't going to mention them now.

"It adds a sense of mystery," I finished, in a more down to earth way.

We all agreed it was a great title for the band. I thought it fitted more than just my band; it seemed to fit my life.

Chapter Four: Sabotage

So, we have a band, two songs and a name. But as anyone sensible knows, that is only 10% of what is needed for a performance. The other 90% taking up all available time, space, money, emotional energy and conversation is what to wear. We didn't exactly have an image, if you know what I mean. We weren't punk, or heavy metal, or country. We were a sort of mixture. Adrian was alright. He is tall and skinny and he never looks pasty and spotty. He's got amazing skin and beautiful hair. Yes, OK, I do think he's really attractive and I like to fantasise that we could go out together, but only because I know it would never happen.

Anyway, he was just going to wear jeans and a tee shirt and look fine. Liam's quite – how do you say – well built. Not exactly fat, but I think he might be when he is middle aged. He's already got quite a beer belly and builder's bum when he wears jeans, so Shareen persuaded him he might be better off in some baggy combats. Shareen has got amazing style sense, probably because she is totally beautiful. Her legs are about six foot long and her figure is incredible. She could wear anything and look fantastic. When I asked her at lunchbreak, after our last rehearsal, she just said we could both wear something sort of sparkly on top and jeans or trousers. Sounds so easy, doesn't it. I decided in my head to enlist Bridie's help. But before I finished the conversation, I did ask:

"Don't you think someone should have a word with George? Can you imagine what he'll turn up in?"

Shareen thought about it for a moment.

"No" she said. "I don't. I think it's really important for everyone just to be themselves. We're musicians, artists. We care about the music and if people are going to judge us by the brand label on our jeans, then I don't want to win

43

anyway. If George turns up in his corduroy trousers, well, that's George and good for him for being an individual."

I felt a bit cross. I had only been trying to help and she was making it sound like I was some sort of really superficial idiot who just cared about appearances. It must have shown on my face, because she added:

"But it was really nice of you to think of it. If you think George may feel awkward, you could always just let him know what Adrian and Liam are wearing."

She was good like that, never left anyone feeling down.

The bell went and I pushed my way down the staircase to get to English. We were meant to have set places in the classrooms, but we had a supply teacher again who never knew where anyone was meant to be. So if I got to the classroom first, Bridie and I could sit at the back and she could help me out on the all important clothes question. She would be late, because just as I spent most lunchtimes in the music room rehearsing at the moment, she was out training for the athletics team. There was a great surge of Year 7s pushing and shouting down the English Department Corridor. We barged into C1 and I was nowhere near the front, when the shrieking voice of Miss Weekly cut through the chaos like a drill.

"Year 7! Year 7! Get out of this room! I have never seen such appalling behaviour in the corridors from Year 7s. If you can't remember how to line up sensibly, you'll have to practice after school. Go on, you boys, get out and line up properly in the corridor."

A lot of teachers are quite sexist, I think. They assume that pushing and swearing and barging around are boy things, and that girls tuck their files under their arms and wait quietly in lines! There may be a tiny miniscule bit of truth in it, but not much. However, I certainly wasn't going to complain! With a smug smile I watched Javaad being sent to the back of the line for no good reason at all other than being one of the male species and I stood smugly at the front, with my best meek and mild female face on.

"Thank you, Ellie," said Miss Weekly. "It's good to know that at least some of you have manners. You may go in now and sit quietly in your proper seats."

With the innocence of some Victorian school girl in those lessons when you see them walking around with books on their heads, I entered the classroom and sat, cunningly, in the one row from the back (back row too obvious) and at the side. Bridie came puffing in at the end of the line and came and sat next to me.

"Good move!" she commented, as she arranged our files and weekly planners in a studious looking pattern over the table. I fished out my most recent copy of Style, which fitted neatly into the text book on Writing to Persuade. The supply teacher didn't have a hope. Toni refused to spit out her chewing gum, he sent her out, she stood outside making faces through the window. Ibrar said he felt sick, left the room and never came back. He did like a little siesta in the park after lunch! Most people just chatted and did no work in a fairly harmless way. George was sitting near the front, reading. Despite our rehearsals, we didn't really communicate when we bumped into each other round school. I felt mean, but he didn't look as though he cared. Was he lonely, I wondered, or happy with his own company?

Lessons like that are a total waste of time. On the whole, I tend to think they are quite fun, a good way of getting out of working, but Chris has got a friend in Year 11 who goes to a school in Helstead which is in a real state and they have supply teachers the whole time which really messes up her GCSEs. It's not giving kids a fair chance when your education is ruined like that, when it's not your fault. They never talk about that on the news, do they, when they run stories about anti-social behaviour and falling standards? Anyway, as far as I was concerned in Period 5 on a Tuesday afternoon in the Summer Term of Year 7, an English lesson is the perfect place for a bit of a fashion discussion – nothing more, nothing less.

"How about that, that's beautiful!" said Bridie pointing to a glossy photo of a black strapless top.

"It would be fine if I had any boobs," I said. "But I'm about as flat chested as a squashed fly. It would simply fall off and that would be entertaining for everyone."

"I don't know. They're getting bigger" Bridie teased. "You'll be able to buy a 28AA soon!"

I kicked her under the table and muttered something about grapefruits, given that Bridie was – how shall I say – pretty well equipped! The supply teacher tried to give a stern, "I'm keeping my eye on you" sort of look as we collapsed into giggles.

We flicked through the pages and Bridie got so exasperated by my negativity that she opened a page of her English book, wrote "Ellie's Fashion Crisis" at the top and then ruled a line down the middle with 'advantages' and 'disadvantages' heading each column. It was one of her habits, making lists in a crisis.

	Advantages	Disadvantages
Black top	sexy	No boobs
Silky dress`	Lovely colour	Shows legs
Mini skirt	V. "in"	Bum too big

Finally, in hilarious exasperation, she wrote:

Sack with plastic bag Over head	Does not show any part of body	Ugly

She illustrated the last item! At which point, Miss Weekly came back in and collected all the English books to mark our work. What work? She was too quick and the Advantages and Disadvantages page disappeared into her marking bag.

"Oops!" I said, but it was too funny to think of Miss Weekly sitting in her lonely flat with a cat and a cup of cocoa (or so we imagined) putting red ink under Bridie's use of punctuation and writing "Do not use slang" next to the word boobs. (Just so you know, you need to be careful about making assumptions about teachers. Last term someone googled our twitchy, shrivelled Head of Geography and discovered she was UK underwater hockey champion – now you'd never have guessed that!).

We made our way to Maths, fashion issue still unresolved. It was going to need a sleepover, so Bridie phoned her mum and got permission to spend the night at my house, going through my less than enormous wardrobe until it was decided that I would wear my new(ish) jeans and the top I had bought for the Fashion, Food and Funk Festival in May. Everyone said I looked really good in it that evening and the picture in the newspaper had been quite reasonable even by my hyper critical standards. It also had the added advantage that Mum could not grumble that I was asking her for yet more money to buy something new. She had already spent money on stuff for Highwood House which was now less than a week away.

Friday - the day of the Battle of the Bands – at last. Everything at school went so slowly I became convinced that the world had stopped turning. I felt too sick with nerves at lunchtime to eat much, but I went to the canteen anyway with

Bridie and Javaad and Hayley just for something to do. I sat pushing the congealed rice and curry round my plate and they looked at the programme for the evening. I caught sight of George, carrying his tray, looking for a spare seat. I don't know why – it must have been my brain was unhinged with nerves and adrenalin, but I waved and he hesitated, then came over.

"Is anyone sitting here?" He asked.

Oh God, right in the middle of the canteen, I thought. It's bad enough everyone seeing us playing together tonight, but at least Adrian and Liam and Shareen will be on stage as well and they have street cred to counteract his nerdishness. But here….it was too late.

"No, sit down. I'm too nervous to eat anything, so I'm not staying long." I said, already making my excuses.

"What are you nervous about?" he asked, quite genuinely.

He was seriously deranged. How could anyone not be nervous when in eight hours time they were going to have to stand up on stage and sing, with a band, in front of hundreds of people and run the risk of letting down the Year 9s who had invited you to join their group? It was a bit like asking someone why they were worried when an intercity train doing 500 miles per hour was coming down the track and you were tied to the rails like a damsel in distress and not a knight in shining armour to be seen.

"Tonight!" I said feebly.

"Oh. Don't worry!" he said in a puzzled sort of way and started arranging the sausages, chips and beans into separate areas on the plate and eating them, systematically, one by one.

Javaad's head was buried in the programme, if it is possible to bury your head in an A4 leaflet and his shoulders were shaking slightly as he tried to stop sniggering out loud. Bridie made a brave effort at conversation.

"There are nine bands," she said. "How many go through to the region finals?"

"Two," I replied. "I think we've got a chance, because those two," I said, pointing at the programme "and that one – the Desert Rats – they're pretty bad. We heard them rehearsing. Then there are a couple we've no idea about, they've kept really low key."

Javaad had now recovered enough to talk. "Patched Up are always good."

Patched Up were quite a long standing band at school who often played at concerts and at our Performing Arts evening.

I shook my head. "Their guitarist, that boy Steve McVeigh in Year 10, he's really talented. But their problem is that their lead vocalist is in the sixth form and is too old to take part. They've had to rope in someone else".

"Probably some pathetic Year 7 girl like you!" laughed Bridie.

"Actually Ellie's not bad at all" said George, totally seriously and Javaad collapsed all over again.

It was all light hearted and cheering me up, when I saw Toni walking past our table. She was with Nicki, her sister in year 9 and they were always trouble. She'd bullied me at the beginning of the year. I am sure you know the sort of thing: invitations to parties which didn't exist, horrible text messages, comments about me on the internet; even just giggling whenever I came into the classroom. To this day, I don't know why they picked on me, but I wasn't a stranger to hatred and violence. There had been plenty of that around when I was small. So, with a bit of help, I'd sorted her out and she hadn't bothered me particularly since. She had moved on to pick on other girls. Angie, for example, had become so miserable she stopped coming to school for about two weeks. The teachers had arranged reconciliation meetings, but to be truthful, Toni never seemed to change.

She just found a new victim. Nicki, her older sister, could be just as bad, but she was on the Town Youth council with me and wasn't too mean when she was on her own.

But they were still their little gang and it seemed that their one big mission in life was to make other people miserable. What's more, they were in a band and would be playing this evening. What's more, people said they were good. Toni was carrying her tray over to 'her corner' of the canteen, but just as she got to our table, she lurched to one side and her can of drink fell off the tray and all over George.

"Oh, Georgy Porgy, I'm so sorry. Oh look, you're all wet! What a shame! I hope it doesn't upset you for tonight. What a gay like you is doing in Battle of Bands is beyond me." And they all went off, cackling like the witches they were.

It was over and they were nicely ensconced with their gang before any of us could think of a quick reply. George solemnly tipped his plate so the orange juice ran off the plate onto the tray. He picked up his paper napkin (does anyone else in the canteen ever take a paper napkin?) and dabbed at the remaining puddles lying between the sausages and the chips.

"Not so different from apple sauce, I suppose," he commented and carried on eating.

I vowed to myself that they were not going to get off that lightly, if I had anything to do with it.

Seven hours later, I was back in school. Mum and Chris were coming to watch and they gave me a lift, but there were so many cars we couldn't even park near the school.

"Oh my God!" I said. "Who are all these people?"

Luckily some of them turned out to be going to the Adult Education Centre next door for a talk on Chinese History. I only know that because an elderly couple wandered into our school hall by mistake and looked as though they were about to have a heart attack. But even so, there were an awful lot of people at the Battle of the Bands.

We had all drawn numbers to see which order we would play in and guess what – we drew number nine. Last! Shareen said she thought that was great, that we had a chance to make a really big impact, but she always does look on the bright side. Liam and Adrian agreed with me: it just meant we had to sit in total agony for another two hours and we would probably have been carted off in an ambulance suffering from nervous exhaustion by the time our turn came. George – well you've guessed it – seemed oblivious.

We all sat in a row towards the back of the school hall. There was a great big banner across the stage saying Battle of the Bands and sitting in front were the judges: Ms Bright our director of Performing Arts, who probably listens to Val Doonican in her spare time (and if you don't know who he is, ask your grandparents and mention rocking chairs and polo neck sweaters); Mr Sheppard, a dad of an ex – pupil who runs a recording studio in London; and JJ, a pretty cool youth worker who runs a project called Dex which takes a mobile recording studio round to clubs and schools. When you come to think about it, they were some pretty serious judges. But I wasn't thinking at the time. My mind was one big blank sheet of nothing.

When the first few bands had gone, I did relax a little. I knew for certain that we were better than at least three of them. The opening group had made an unbelievable amount of noise, but I'm not sure even I could say it was music. I looked over my shoulder and I could see Mum was maybe regretting coming. I should have provided free ear plugs. The next two had one or two people in the group who were obviously really good, but they sounded weak as though they did not really believe in themselves. After the interval, we all agreed that VoiceOver, which had Camilla Heard as their lead vocalist were the main contenders.

Patched Up – as we predicted – were pretty impressive as far as the instrumentals go, but I felt sorry for Jamie who sang because everyone was going to compare him to Paddy who was too old to compete and to be honest, there was just no comparison. We went backstage to get ready because there was just one more band before us - Looking Black.

It's a pretty bleak name and a pretty bleak collection of people. Nicki was singing with her boyfriend, David, who also played electric guitar, with Toni and two others supporting them. Dave's a seriously scary figure who is often excluded from school. Some people say he's stoned half the time, others say that he never touches drugs himself, just deals in them and makes loads of money out of other people. I could tell from the exchanged glances between the Head and some of the teachers in the audience that they weren't happy that Dave was competing at all. I guess they would not want him representing our school in any regional finals. But, to be fair, he has an incredible voice and there was something wild and edgy in their performance that made your heart race. When their last drum roll had finished, I could see through the cracks in the black out curtains that people in the audience were standing up, stamping their feet and cheering.

I couldn't see Toni as the band left the stage, but then I caught sight of her still out front, scrabbling around on the floor. Perhaps she had dropped something.

I didn't give it a second thought.

We had a five minute set up time while the judges recorded their thoughts on Looking Black and then it was us. We had done some vocal warm ups in the music room, Liam had tuned the guitar and George had played a whole load of scales on a practice keyboard that made it sound as though he was about to perform some Bach concerto in the Royal Albert Hall. Adrian had been tapping all night, so he hardly needed to warm up.

What if I forget the words.

What if I can't reach the high notes.

What if I get stage fright and can't sing at all.

What if everyone thinks I'm rubbish.

What if I let everyone else down.

What if....

Why, why, why did I ever think I could do this?

But then before I could think of an answer, I heard the announcement.

"And now, the last act of this evenings Battle of the Bands – Glass Darkly! Give them a big hand!"

The curtain drew back and we stood blinking into the lights. I couldn't see anything, but I could certainly hear Bridie's voice amongst all the cheering. We waited for Adrian to give the first hit on the high hat to get things started. My mouth was dry. My breathing was so shallow I thought I might faint. And we waited. And we waited.

Shareen half turned round. Adrian was bending over, looking at the stage floor.

"Where are my drum sticks?" he whispered loudly, panic in his voice. "I put them right here."

I could hear myself breathing. The audience started murmuring. Shareen, so much more composed than me, left the mic and went back to help him look.

"Do we have a problem?" asked Andy, the Head Boy who was the "front man" for the evening.

"My drum sticks. I put them here ready to play, just before the curtain went up." I could hear the panic in Adrian's tight voice. .

"Well, I've heard of people having to ask if there is a Doctor in the house, but never if there is a drummer!" joked

Andy to the restless audience, trying to keep the show moving. But then he said "Oh, you might just be in luck, guys, are these what you are looking for?" and he reached down and picked up a pair of drum sticks which looked as though they must have rolled down the stage, towards his stand.

Relief. Then horror. When he held them up, it was clear that they had been snapped, deliberately snapped.

"What the......," but Andy stopped himself swearing just in time – the microphones were on, after all! "Sorry folks, but I think we are going to take two minutes, sort out some new drum sticks for Glass Darkly and then start all over again."

He signalled for the curtain to be lowered.

Adrian was just standing, holding the smashed drumsticks. "I don't understand..... they were fine...who could have...?"

I felt tears welling up in my eyes, Liam was kicking the speaker in anger, George stood impassively (in his corduroys) at the keyboard. Shareen caught my eye. We were both thinking the same thing. The only people who could have done this, would have done this, were the people on stage before us. Or someone who had been clearing the stage. That was what Toni had been doing. My nerves and tears turned to anger, so strong I wanted to push past the curtain, grab the mic and let everyone know what an evil person she was.

"What bad luck!" I heard Ms Hensome saying, out of breath. She had rushed back over to her music room and come back with another pair of drumsticks. "They're probably not as good as yours, but they're certainly in better shape than these," she said, trying to lighten things up.

Then she added, more seriously, "Listen, you have more musical talent in this one band than all the rest put together. You go out there and prove it. Show them!"

It was what we all needed. I felt the rage and fear in me turn to something else, something stronger and more powerful. A desire to sing, to perform and to show them all that no-one was going to stop Glass Darkly.

And no-one did! When it came to the results, JJ said that the judges had been unanimous in their first choice. It was a band that demonstrated originality, energy and ability. It was a band with an extremely talented lead singer. It was a band that had the ability to go on and win the regionals, if not the finals! It was – yes – Glass Darkly!

Even George did a little hop! I flung myself at Adrian and burst into tears and then felt hideously embarrassed for the rest of the evening. Liam and Shareen hugged each other. We had done it!

The only thing that spoiled the evening at all was that Looking Black came second. It seemed unfair when they had tried to sabotage our performance and I felt my heart sink when their name was announced as the other band going through to the regional finals. It seemed our bitter rivalry was only just beginning.

Chapter Five: The Locked Room

A professor told a newspaper recently that it was inhuman to make teenagers get out of bed and start school at 8.45 because our bodies and brains are programmed to lie in bed until about midday and that we didn't start functioning until the afternoon. Now that's the sort of person who should have a Nobel prize. That's what I call sensible advice. Not that any parents or teachers seemed to take any notice of it. So, whenever I get the opportunity, I remain in a coma in my wonderful, lovely, comfortable, delicious bed for as long as I can. The morning after the Battle of the Bands, it was 12.30 before I even opened my eyes. The dreams of the ghostly children had been replaced by dreams of fame and wealth and celebrity!

Eating a sort of brunch, mum asked me what had gone on at the beginning of the act. I told her that the drum sticks had been deliberately broken, presumably to put us off, and that it must have been Toni.

"Oh no!" she said. "Not the same crowd who you had all that trouble with last year?"

"Yes, them," I scowled.

"But I thought you got on OK at the Festival," said Mum. "You must learn to put disagreements behind you."

"Who are you preaching at now?" I asked crossly. Why does she always assume that I have done something wrong? "We didn't start this. I don't like them and Nicki's boyfriend is a complete loser, but we didn't do anything. What am I supposed to do about it if they try to wreck our chances in the competition?"

"No, you're right," she agreed. "But try not to get sucked into some long running quarrel. There are more important things in life, you know..." Then she went on, brightly, in her sort of "let's not get into an argument" voice. "Now, what about packing for Highwood? You're leaving on Monday."

I went over to Bridie's in the afternoon to help her sort out her stuff. Her mum made a delicious apple cake and we stuffed ourselves until we thought that we probably wouldn't be able to tackle any obstacle course because the equipment would collapse under our weight. She's very homely like that, Bridie's mum. Always making things, helping Bridie do her hair, changing the duvet covers. Maybe its because she stays at home (that's where she does her childminding) and my mum goes out to work, but when she hugs me she feels like ....well, homely. Plump, bosomy (if that's a word, but I am sure you know what I mean) and homely. A real mum.

Not *my* real mum, you understand, but *a* real mum. Perhaps the sort of mother I used to dream of, looking through picture books in day care centres and foster homes, mums pushing swings, Dads taking you to school holding your hand, both of them together unwrapping birthday presents on the floor of a sunny sitting room. Do I sound ungrateful? I wouldn't swap my adoptive mum and dad for anything now – they have stuck with me through thick and thin, but that does not mean to say that Bridie's mum wasn't special too.

"You're as thin as a rake, Ellie Long," she laughed squeezing me. "You better have some more apple cake otherwise we won't even be able to see you on stage in your band. You'll have disappeared," and somehow, whenever she spoke, she sounded as though she was singing.

She wanted to give Bridie all this food to take to Highwood "just in case they don't know how to cook properly", but Bridie objected, saying it was far too embarrassing to turn up with a suitcase full of apple cake and bananas. Part of me wanted to disagree. Food is very, very important to me, but Bridie did have a point. Having got rid of the wartime rations idea, we managed to get Bridie's luggage down to one enormous suitcase which contained everything except her Wellington boots, her coat and her wash and make-up bag. I told you she was going to need a whole separate trunk for that.

I repeated the exercise myself at home on the Sunday, after lunch, but being someone used to moving on and moving around, I squashed all my gear into one holdall. I ticked off everything on the list, double checked it with Mum and went downstairs to crash out in front of the television. I don't mind saying that I am a bit of a telly addict, although I do try to be a bit disciplined. It is amazing how much of a day over half term can disappear watching Daytime Make a Million or Your New House or – even better – My Girlfriend Loves My Brother – What shall I do?" And that's not even taking account of the soaps. I have been warned on many occasions: you may become an expert on DIY but you're unlikely to pass your GCSEs and you'll certainly never earn enough money to buy The House of Your Dreams (BBC Tuesdays 11am!).

The sun was just setting, late in the day and Dad had cleared up his gardening tools. Despite the roses infested with greenfly and the moth eaten lettuces, he does like to fancy himself as a bit of a green fingered marvel. Chris came back from his run. Bending over on the low brick wall outside the open patio door, and stretching out his legs one by one, he gasped.

"I saw those ponies again. Ellie, are you listening?"

"What?" I said, glued to Kitchen Queen and a recipe for cheese soufflé, oblivious to the fact that I almost never cook!

"Well, if you're not interested......" he said, knowing exactly what buttons to press.

"No, I am. Sorry. What did you say? This is rubbish anyway," I said, turning off the TV with the remote and sending the grinning chef and his gormless assistant into the black hole of the blank screen.

"I just said," repeated Chris, sounding more middle aged by the minute, "that I saw those ponies again, you know the ones you were so upset about."

"Oh no!" I cried. "How were they? Were they still tied up?"

"Yep. I see what you were talking about now. I think it's probably worse now, if anything," Chris said. "The farmer didn't seem to be around, so I took a closer look. They're pretty thin and the headcollar is really digging into the flesh on the smaller one. I don't know much about ponies, but they didn't look too happy to me."

How could I have been so selfish? I had been so wrapped up in my own stuff, with the band and going to Highwood, that I hadn't even thought about the ponies. I had meant to go for a walk at the weekend and check them out, but what had I done instead? Spent hours organising make up, and trying on my sweatshirt to make sure I looked nice for some pathetic school outing and then spent two hours in front of the telly. All that anger I had felt a couple of weeks ago, looking on the websites, arguing with mum, all that had come to nothing.

Mum and Dad were going to church and on to some charity event, so I knew I might not get a chance to speak to them in the evening and the next morning was going to be a rush. We had to be at school for the coach at 7.30. So I wrote a note and put it on the kitchen table.

Mum - In case I forget, please, please, please ring the Horse Rescue centre about the ponies at Middle Farm. Chris says they're really bad now. Ask him for details. x Ellie

Which made me feel a bit better, but not much. I went to bed and slept badly. Sometimes when I woke in the mornings it seemed as though every night now was filled with vivid dreams and when I woke up in the mornings I hardly knew what was true and what was not. That night was no different. Somehow the band and the ponies and the activity week were all mixed up together and there was a baby crying, crying all the time, sitting in the garden. And just like I never seemed to be able to give the children playing in the alley whatever it was they needed, nor could I stop the baby crying. I don't know if dreams can show you the future or deal with the past, but when I thought about them in daylight, the name of the band made more and more sense. "Now we see through Glass Darkly….."

All of which meant a restless night and I felt like death in the morning. Getting to school for a coach at 7.30 meant leaving home by 7.00. Leaving home by 7.00 meant getting up by 6.15. Getting up at 6.15 was hell. But I coped. Just. With much panic, a cold shower because the hot water hadn't come on and a rather pathetic breakfast because the milkman hadn't been, I leapt in the car and Dad took me in. Quite a few people were at school already, milling around in the car park, some with parents, some without.

"Its OK Dad, you can just drop me off," I reassured him. I knew he wanted to get off to work and I certainly didn't want him hanging around and waving goodbye. He never talks to any of the other adults and stands around looking embarrassing.

"If you're sure…" He was clearly relieved. He kissed me and drove off, one hand out of the window waving goodbye. Not so different from the pictures in the children's books then, I thought wryly to myself. I am lucky to have found a mum and dad like them.

Everyone was standing around in groups. I was surprised to see George, but I was much better at standing up for myself (and him) now, since winning the band competition and I went over to chat to him.

"Hi George! I was totally wiped out after Friday night, I slept 'till twelve. How about you?"

"I don't really get a chance," he replied. "My little brother wakes us up early."

I was surprised. He had never mentioned any brothers or sisters before and I had always imagined him as an only child.

"I didn't think this was your sort of thing, assault courses and team building," I joked.

"It's not really," he admitted. "My Dad thought it would be good for me to get away for a few days."
"Get away from what? The office?"

But there was something slightly odd about George's silence, so I dropped the subject and said goodbye, having just seen Bridie arriving with her mega luggage. Javaad came up to join us with Lewis and Salim. Lewis always seems sort of quiet at school, especially around girls. Someone told me he has four brothers and lives with his grandfather, his dad and his poor mum. Imagine the ratio 6:1! Poor woman! Anyway, that may explain why he always looks as though he's blushing whenever he is in close proximity to a girl! Salim, on the other hand, is the total opposite.

"Hi Bridie, what have you got in your tiny little suitcase there?"

"Mind your own business! What have you got in yours?" Bridie retorted, quick as a flash.

"I'm sure I could give you a glimpse of my possessions if you come up to my dormitory!" smirked Salim.

Luckily the bus arrived and Salim had to stop his pathetic attempts to chat us up! We all cheered, climbed on board and set off, the five of us spread out along the back seat! Highwood wasn't that far, but given the traffic, it took over an hour and we turned in the gates at about 9.30.

"Enter a Different World" I thought to myself.

The coach wound its way up a long drive, flanked by ancient oaks standing like soldiers guarding the idyllic parkland which stretched into the distance. Apart from the SLOW signs and humps in the road, it could have been a hundred years ago and we could have been arriving in a coach and four. Round the last bend, the house came into view.

It was a fantastic old stately home, made from mellow stone that glowed in the morning summer sun. In the centre of the immaculate circular lawn in front of the grand porch was an old fountain, with a child holding up a jug from which poured cool, pure water. The gravel scrunched under our feet when we got out of the coach and even though everyone was shouting and laughing, you could still hear the birds as they flew in and out of a dovecote to the left of the house. I thought it was truly a magical place and I was under its spell from the moment I saw it.

"Wake up, Ellie!" said Lewis. "We're going to our rooms."

As it turned out, we weren't allowed to use the front entrance, so we all went round the side of the house where there was a more modern, rather ugly ground floor extension. Josh, the Highwood leader, explained that all outdoor shoes got left there.

"This is an amazing building," he explained "and we are really privileged to have it as a young person's activity centre, but we have to look after it. Inside you will see, there are still lots of the original floors and wooden panelling, as well as a beautiful oak staircase which dates right back to the 16th century. So we can't have you lot demolishing four hundred years of history in three days!"

We kicked off our shoes and then went into the main part of the house. There was a huge hall and the first thing that struck you, in between the notice boards and fire regulations, was an enormous painting of a pale-faced lady dressed all in green, whose eyes seemed to follow your movements and reach into your soul.

"She is one freaky dame!" said Salim, and for once I had to agree with him.

"That's the Green Lady and she's more freaky than you can even dream of," said Josh, over hearing us, "but that story is for another day."

"Oh, I suppose she haunts the house when it's a full moon!" and Javaad ran howling round the hall with his white tee shirt pulled up over his face.

"You may laugh, my boy, you may laugh!" smiled Josh, but I thought the smile wasn't quite 100%, if you know what I mean.

Upstairs, we separated. The boys were led off by Mr Heath and Josh to the annex, where their dormitories were. Ms Midler, from school and Ali, another one of the Highwood leaders, took us girls along the landing.

"Now, as I explained at school," said Ms Midler, clutching loads of paperwork and a list on a clipboard, "you girls sleep in the bedrooms along this landing, and that corridor down there. Some rooms are for two, some for three and the biggest are for four."

Ali added, "We have a small group of primary children with physical and learning disabilities staying in the specially adapted annex, but otherwise you are the only school here this week. So you are using all the rooms on this landing, except the one on the right at the top of the stairs, and that stays locked."

"Thanks Ali!" said Ms Midler. "I'm sure we'll all respect which rooms are out of bounds and I'll go through that again at the Welcome Meeting in half an hour. In the meantime, I know you girls sorted out who was with who last week, so I'll just read out the names and it should all work out. Fingers crossed."

On the whole, it was a great group who had signed up for Highwood. No sign of any of the bitchy girls like Toni and her gang, thank goodness. Hayley had put down to be in a foursome with Louise, Megan and Amy, so they were pretty happy when their names were called out for one of the larger rooms. Bridie and I had obviously asked to be together and we punched the air when we heard we had got a room for two. Not that we're anti-social or anything like that, but it is nice to have a bit of privacy to gossip about everyone else!

"This is so perfect!" said Bridie, dragging her suitcase into our little room, where two single beds were squashed against the walls, separated by a bedside table and a lamp. There was a cupboard in the corner and some shelves and that was about it. But who needs more? Duvets, duvet covers and sheets were folded in piles on the ends of the mattresses ready for us to make up the beds, but we were far too excited to do anything so mundane.

"Look out of the window!"

I joined Bridie and together we stared at the view out over the emerald lawn, the fountain with the stone child and on, over the peaceful parkland.

"It's like having our own palace!" she exclaimed.

Suddenly, there was the sound of a loud gong being hit downstairs. The deep brass sound echoed round the high ceilings and long corridors of the old building and made us jump out of skins.

"Talk about Hammer House of Horrors!" shrieked Bridie, clutching me.

We grabbed our things and hurried off downstairs for the welcome meeting, where we were going to sign up for different activities for the three days. Half way down the stairs, I remembered I hadn't got my activity sheet which we had been given in advance.

I asked Bridie to save me a place and ran back to our bedroom. Now there were some advantages to having squashed everything in one holdall (for instance, I was actually able to walk up the stairs without having to ask half of the Highwood staff to help me, like Bridie), but equally it meant everything was a complete mess. I chucked all my spare clothes, pants, diary, washbag, squashed frog, out onto the bed before finally finding the Activity Sheet at the very bottom of the bag. Typical. I stuffed it in the pocket of my jeans, slammed the door behind me and hurried down the landing.

Someone was coming up the stairs. A woman. Wearing a long green dress. Not an ordinary woman. I hesitated. I smiled. But she did not acknowledge me. She turned and went straight into the locked room. Without opening the door.

Chapter Six: Intruders

When I got to the main hall where the Welcome Meeting was being held Josh was running through a powerpoint with some basic rules and the outline of the visit, but it made no impression on my mind. They were just lines and meaningless words on a piece of paper. All I could think of was the lady I had just seen on the stairs. Had I seen her? Yes, I was sure I had. With just the same feeling as when I saw those kids playing at the B&B when I was so young, or the park-keeper, or the shepherd. Or more recently, the children in the sunlit wood....were they becoming more frequent, these visits from another world?

"Ellie!" Bridie nudged me. "Concentrate! We've got to choose our activities now!"

I shook myself and decided not to say anything just yet, so I forced myself to look at the list. Most activities took a whole morning or a whole afternoon.

Lake activities:	sailing, raft building, canoeing, windsurfing
Other outdoor:	horse riding, ropes and assault course, problem solving, football
Indoor:	drama, art and music

Initially, we all grouped together and tried to work out what we could all do. Then Javaad pointed out that what we were doing was pointless.

"We came here so we could all do stuff we enjoyed, but still be together in free time and the evenings."

"Javaad's right!" I said. "Let's all just choose what we really want to do. Nearly everyone here is OK, so it's not like we're going to be stuck with a whole load of losers whoever we end up with."

I looked at the list, still feeling a bit wobbly and not totally concentrating. It was a beautiful day outside; the sun was hot and the sky looked clear. If there was going to be a day when it would be fun to try watersports then it would be today. I had tried canoeing before and ended up with blisters and a sore bum, so I ruled that out. Noticing the leaves on the avenue of oaks fluttering, I decided windsurfing looked good. So I put a big tick in that column.

Tuesday I knew I wanted to try riding, so that was the morning sorted. I would join a beginners group so at least I wouldn't look too stupid and apparently they had a sort of indoor riding school so at least no four legged maniac could charge away with me over the horizon. Ticking that column made me think of the ponies at home. I realised that the note I had left on the kitchen table was no good. Chris was off to France on his school trip and I was sure they would not have had time to discuss the ponies. That meant they would be left there another whole week, tied up and suffering in the heat, all because of my selfishness.

"I've put riding for tomorrow morning," I said to Bridie. "I probably won't even be able to walk in the afternoon, so I am going to put Music for after lunch and hope it's not some ghastly choir event."

Bridie laughed. "Has anyone got as far as Wednesday morning yet? "

Nobody had. So she suggested we all did something together on the last morning.

"Great idea, Bridie" said Salim, who was looking increasingly like he was going to worship everything Bridie ever did or said. "You choose!"

I giggled and Bridie gave me a stare. I giggled even more and caught Lewis' eye, which set him off as well. Javaad, whose radar was often a bit weak on relationships, didn't get it at all. He just looked puzzled and suggested the ropes course.

"Sounds good!" We agreed and we all ticked that for Wednesday morning and Javaad scribbled a note on the bottom of his form saying that, if possible, we would like to be together on that activity.

So, everything was organised. But I had this strange feeling that I could tick all the boxes and make all the plans in the world, and then something unexpected would come along, or something else wouldn't turn out the way you expected, and its all change. The pale lady in the green dress did not fit into any box on any timetable.

"Before we finish," said Josh, quietening everyone down, "let me run through a few rules about the house and garden. As I think you have been told, the room at the top of the stairs on the left (as you are going up) is locked and is out of bounds. Please don't try to break in."

"Why?" called out Hayley, putting up her hand.

"It's a long story," said Josh, "and maybe I'll have time to tell you before you leave. But this house was left to the Youth Foundation by the family who had lived here for hundreds of years and it was one of their only requests that that particular bedroom was left undisturbed. It seems only fair to honour it, I am sure you'll agree.

And in the same way, there is still one part of the garden which is out of bounds. If you walk past the fountain with the little girl on the top, you will see a wrought iron gate between two high hedges. That leads into a small rose garden which is private, again because that is what the original owners wanted.

The lake and the stables are out of bounds, unless you are with an adult, for safety reasons. You cannot try out any of the equipment like the assault course or the climbing wall unless you are on an organised activity with an adult.

Otherwise, you are free to wander anywhere, as long as you respect the beauty and peace of the place and stay safe. As the Americans say, take only photographs, leave only footprints. Sound reasonable?"

"Yep!" we all agreed.

"Good! Then you have about 30 minutes to get yourself a drink and a snack from the canteen and sort out your rooms – and no! There is no-one else to make your beds! You'll find your groups for the welcome activity on the main noticeboard by the boot and shoe racks and you need to be outside, ready for action, in old clothes by 11.10. And," he finished jokingly, "expect the unexpected!"

I thought privately to myself that I had already met the unexpected. I thought about saying something to Josh because he seemed a really approachable person. And although he must do this with hundreds of groups every year, he also managed to look and sound really enthusiastic. I hesitated.

"Are you OK? You look a bit puzzled," he said to me.

That was putting it mildly, I thought.

"No! I'm fine, thanks!" and the opportunity passed.

"Great. See you outside then!" and off he went.

He looked as though he really loved his job and as I went to find the others, I found myself hoping that I end up with a job which does some good, is as much fun as his and which I really enjoy. I don't expect Josh earned much money – but he was happy and money isn't everything.

If I couldn't talk to him, I had to talk to someone otherwise I was going to burst. So I intercepted Bridie on her way to the canteen.

"Let's get our room done first" I said to Bridie, pushing her towards the stairs.

"That doesn't sound like you, putting tidiness before food," she said. "I'm starving. I had breakfast at 6am this morning!"

"I need to talk to you!" I said, half whispering and she must have seen the look on my face because she changed direction and followed me. As we climbed the wide, curving stairs, running my hand on the smooth oak banister, I slowed down and gulped.

"Listen, I was coming back with my activity sheet, you know when you had gone on ahead and, and – well, I saw someone coming up the stairs and going into the locked room."

"What?" asked Bridie. "Who?"

"I don't know."

"Well, maybe some of the staff are allowed in there, just to open the windows and dust, that sort of thing."

"No, you don't understand," I said. By this time, we were standing outside the room itself. "She went into this room, but she didn't open the door. She went straight through it!"

Bridie just looked at me. She wrinkled up her eyebrows and stared, first at me, then at the door.

"You're freaking me out!"

"Look!" I pointed at the round, brass door handle which had a thin layer of dust on it, "there are no finger prints. And here…" I ran my hand down the solid, dark wood panels, "there is a cobweb here which hasn't been broken. The door was not opened and I am not joking."

"Well then you must have been mistaken and she can't have gone in that room," Bridie insisted.

A few of the girls were now coming up from the canteen, munching biscuits and chatting.

"Is that the locked room?" asked Maya. "Sounds spooky to me. I'm staying well clear."

Hayley agreed. "I'm glad our room is the other end of the landing. I think the owner must have left a body in the chest!" and they shrieked and ran off down the corridor.

"Come on!" I said to Bride and we went back to our bedroom.

We sat on our beds, with the sun streaming through the window and lighting a faint ray of dust hanging in the air. Then I told her that I had seen – others – ghosts – before and that I was pretty sure that this lady I had seen, in the long green dress was another. She looked a bit shocked because she could tell I was serious, but also, understandably, a bit sceptical.

"Do you think it was that lady in the portrait downstairs? The one in the green dress?" she asked.

"To tell you the truth, I don't know. I couldn't even really tell you how old fashioned she looked. Or what her face looked like. Her hair, it was long, sort of hanging down over her face. The whole thing only lasted maybe two seconds."

We discussed what to do – if anything – while we made the beds and put some of our clothes away on the shelves and our washbags on the windowsill. With the sunlight behind her, the child on the fountain seemed to be beckoning us outside. We agreed in the end to try to ask a few questions about the lady in the portrait and the locked room and see if we could understand the whole thing a bit better. But we both also agreed not to mention what I had seen. Bridie, I think, because she only half believed it. Me, because I believed it only too strongly.

The gong went again. We had missed the drink and biscuits and as we peered down the landing on our way out, there was not sign of any wailing headless ghosts or wandering spirits. Bridie gave me a sort of "Well? Where is she now?" look and we walked, just a bit faster than usual, past the room, down the stairs and off to the meeting point for the Welcome Activity.

Which proved to be hilarious. If you have ever tried working with five others, including Javaad, Salim and Lewis and moving a chest across a "swamp" using only two planks, four tyres and four ropes then you will know what I mean. I expect you have done that sort of exercise. They do them on most trips, but I still think they are great. You really get to see people's characters. Thinking about it, perhaps I would like to be a psychiatrist or psychologist when I leave school, rather than a Youth Leader? So here is my psycho-analysis, with my own personal rating system!

1. Salim – he was Mr Bright Idea. He thought he knew exactly what to do immediately and started heaving planks and tyres around before anyone else had even had time to think. So everyone followed his plan, which was hopeless and resulted in us all getting sent back to the beginning. What did he do then? He sulked, of course. Sulked, until he ended up wedged on the plank at close quarters with Bridie next to him. Then, surprise, surprise, he cheered up!
2/10

2. Bridie – she is a listener. So she put up with Salim's bossiness, then when we all started again, she listened to Javaad's ideas, suggested a few improvements and encouraged everyone else along the way. Which is the kind of person you need if you were stuck with a bomb on top of a crocodile infested swamp.
10/10 (OK – I'm biased!)

3. Lewis would be useful in those circumstances as well, because he gets on and does stuff. The boring bits

like tying decent knots on the tyres so we don't lose our grip on them. People like him don't really get recognised in life, but life would be pretty dreadful without them.
8/10

4. Javaad – he's quite a born leader, I think. I knew that when we worked together on the Youth council and organised the Festival in Canterton last year. Although he can get a bit stroppy at times, he's got a great ability to get people going and following him. He came up with the idea of raising and lowering the planks with the ropes and building small bridges, one at a time. It worked, as well. He was modest at the end, but I could tell he was really pleased.
9/10

5. And me? I don't know. It's always hardest to analyse yourself honestly isn't it? They say a lot of these exercises are sort of trust exercises. You have to be able to touch other people, hold them, take hands with them, and allow them to support you. And, to be honest, I am not sure that I find any of those things very easy. I believed from a young age that the only person who was ever really going to stick with me, was me, so I when push comes to shove, I rely on me. Truthfully, that's not a good philosophy, and I think I am getting better at allowing other people to help me, but I still have a tendency to yell "Get off me!" and "Let go!" and to Salim "Get your filthy hands off me, you pervert" and so on! But at least I made everyone laugh (I am good at that) and that always helps.
?/10 – you can be the judge!

You can probably imagine the mess we got into, but it was great fun and we did manage it in the end. I took about ten photos of us, covered in mud, arms linked and waving like lunatics at the camera, with Salim holding the "bomb" above Javaad's head. Then another with us all pointing at Lewis and holding our noses because – well, as he's a boy I'm sure you can guess why! And a third with everyone lying flat on the floor with stupid faces pretending to be collapsed through exhaustion.

That's the good thing about digital cameras; you can take a ridiculous amount of ridiculous pictures. The bad thing is that once I've downloaded them and sent them to everyone, I always forget to get any printed. So you can never exactly sit down and flick through them, or stare at them for a long time, remembering, wondering. Like I do from time to time with my zoo /giraffe /mother photo.

Lunch was pretty ordinary, but I was so ravenous by then that I would have eaten anything at all! I think it was because I ate so much that I was totally unable to stay afloat on my windsurfer for more than two seconds in the afternoon. This was what I wrote in my Highwood diary.

Afternoon – windsurfing. Never again! I have swallowed so much of the lake that there will be no watersports for the rest of the summer! The lake is empty! It looks easy – but it's not. I think God designed me as a land animal.

Which just about sums it up really!

We all met up again at supper. Bridie had really enjoyed herself sailing. I had seen her (on the rare moments when I surfaced) speeding across the lake, leaning right out from the tiny sailing boat. The instructor had said she was a natural and should try to take it up.

"Easier said than done," she grumbled, "when we live in a town that is as far from the sea as anywhere in England!"

The boys had done football, which was not exactly inspiring, but they all seemed excited that the coach was some ex Man U player and I guess it's whatever turns you on! We were just finishing seconds of sponge pudding and ice cream when Ali got up and banged on the table.

"Just when you thought you couldn't take any more...." She paused for effect. "Now for the Treasure Hunt!"

There was a confused roar which combined groans of exhaustion, whoops of fake joy and howls of hysterical laughter. Our poor 21 century i-pod, tv, computer game bodies were not used to such a ceaseless round of physical activity.

"You will need to be in teams of 3- No! Please don't all start sorting that out now, otherwise I'll never finish explaining how it runs. All I'll say is, make sure you don't leave anyone out. I'll give each team the sheet of clues. All you have to do is to work out the answer. When you find the location, there will be a post with a number on it. You have to write that number where it says "answer" on the sheet. It is your proof that you solved the clue.

If you have any problems, or anyone has an accident, remember the rule. One person stays with the casualty, the other comes here, to the house, to get help. There will be plenty of staff based here and wandering about, so you needn't worry. Any questions? Good. Now, you must follow the usual rules about safety and out of bounds – like the rose garden, for instance. And you must be back here, in the main hall to hand in your sheets and have hot chocolate by 9.0'clock."

We were given five minutes to sort out our teams. Salim suggested (I can't think why?!) that we split up as boys and girls and that he and Lewis went with Bridie. That left just Javaad and I, so we needed a third person.

"What about George? He looks a bit lonely," Javaad. pointed out.

I looked over at George and was suddenly aware how sad he seemed at times. He is quite small for his age and his blonde hair flops quite unfashionably over his face, hiding his brown eyes which are actually quite attractive. I overheard a teacher once confiding in my mum in the playground that she thought I seemed older than my years although I looked younger than I was. At the time, I couldn't fathom what she was on about, but seeing George alone, but surrounded by fifty people, the phrase made sense. He looked as though he carried the cares of the world on his shoulders and I felt sad for him. Salim's jeering voice broke through my thoughts.

"You won't get far if you have to run round the park with that lump."

And because he said that, and because he was starting to annoy me, and because I thought it was unfair to judge George like that (despite the fact that was exactly what I had done the first time he turned up to rehearsals), I said, "Great idea Javaad, I'll go and ask him." So I pushed my way across the canteen and tapped him on the shoulder.

"Do you want to come with me and Javaad?" I asked.

He looked relieved to have been rescued from that "person who hasn't got a team" predicament and I realised he probably wasn't as self-contained as he appeared.

We collected our sheet, the gong went again and we were off on the count of three. We skimmed down the clues and spotted a couple we could do quite quickly.

"This one's easy," I said. "It must the door to the back annex where we put our filthy shoes." And sure enough we ran there and noted down the number on the post, just by the bootscraper.

77

"01539" I read out to Javaad, who had the pencil and sheet.

"Good work," he said, "what's next?"

"How about number 4?"

That one led us to the croquet lawn! I've never played croquet but I remembered it from a play of Alice in Wonderland we had done as our leavers' production in Year 6. Clue Number eight was in the middle of a circle of tall pine trees behind the football pitches. Hayley, Rachel and Amy were sprawled on the grass there, chatting and they helpfully pointed us in the direction of number nine which was a beautiful summer house overlooking the lake. They are not the competitive type! There were just two clues left and we were feeling quite smug about our progress.

I read out number nine.

"When frost nips the leaves and there's snow on the ground
Grapes, melons and peppers in here will be found"

"Greenhouses!" said Javaad. "I saw them when we were on our way to the swamp activity this afternoon. Come on!"

We didn't go too fast, because George was trying his hardest to run fast, but was now totally puffed out! He just wasn't built to be an Olympic athlete. He caught up with us as we were admiring the line of greenhouses, built up against a tall red brick wall.

"Do you know," George said "that they used to have mini boiler houses where they employed boys to keep the fires burning. They heated up the wall and the wall heated up the greenhouses which meant they could grow all these exotic fruits and flowers."

"How do you know all this stuff?" I asked.

"I'm reading a book set in a house like this in Victorian times. There would probably have been about 50 servants in a place like this. Not just gardeners, but laundry workers, stable lads, maids, a governess......" He tailed off, seeming a little embarrassed by his knowledge.

We stood quietly, imagining the place as it must have been in those times. Javaad shivered.

"Its weird," he said "it's almost like you can still feel them here, as if we are invading their place."

I looked at him. Did he really mean that? Had he seen something to make him think that? Like I had?

We recorded the number on the post and George leant over Javaad's shoulder and read out the next clue.

In the East I rise, in the West I fall
Again tomorrow will I call.

"What the heck?" said Javaad.

"It's probably a sundial, if you think about it," said George, slowly. "Old houses like this usually had them in the gardens. There's one in this book I'm reading. It's built at a sort of crossroads, where the garden paths meet, in the middle of an orchard."

We racked our brains to see if we had seen anything like that, but although by now we had been pretty much over the whole grounds, we had not seen a sundial.

George continued, thinking out loud. "Let's follow this gravel path. It's going through the kitchen gardens where they grow vegetables and look, it goes through a hedge at the other end. We haven't been that way, I am sure."

So we followed George, past wigwams of tangling runner beans growing up bamboo poles, rows of glowing green lettuces, rhubarb plants with great pre-historic sized leaves

79

and bushes hanging heavy with blackcurrants and gooseberries. Javaad tried to pick one and pricked his finger.

"Serves you right for stealing!" I joked and popped a cherry tomato in my mouth at the same time!

"Try one of these,"

George held out a few pods in his hand and we split them open and picked out the tiny peas which were incredibly sweet and fresh. Javaad stared at the empty pods and commented on how many you would need to fill a bag of frozen peas! It was an extra-ordinary thought and we all laughed. But seriously, although you may think this is weird, I found the vegetable garden beautiful – quite beautiful! Everything was orderly and natural at the same time; the food looked like real food, not all wrapped up in ten layers of plastic like you see in supermarkets. We stood, mesmerised as if we were standing in the Garden of Eden, before taking the path to the end of the kitchen garden and reaching a small arch sculptured out of a dark, yew hedge...

"Are we meant to be here?" Javaad asked, uncertainly. "It doesn't look like the rest of the grounds."

George peered through the gap and then stepped through. We followed him. We found ourselves in a small, totally enclosed garden. The smell of roses overpowered the summer evening and filled the warm air and bewitched us, leaving us drowsy and drugged with the heavy scent. There were roses everywhere. Wild white roses climbing haphazardly up the old red brick wall at the far end of the garden; small, delicate pink roses winding their way through the branches of the gnarled apple trees; great bushes of blood red roses, grouped in the centre flower bed surrounding a small pond where they were reflected in the dark, still water. The light was fading and the roses seemed to shine through the evening mist. It was completely silent.

Almost completely silent.

In the stillness, I heard the sound of a child laughing. Children maybe. It was difficult to tell. She, he, they sounded as though they were running, playing. Was it just me? I looked at Javaad, but it seemed that he had not heard anything. But George turned and we stared straight at each other. I knew, I just knew, that he too had heard the invisible children.

All three of us, simultaneously, turned to leave. George said what we were all thinking.

"We are intruders here!"

Chapter Seven: A Lost Child

Sleep crept round the edge of my bed all night, like a skulking hound unwilling to be caught, always just out of reach. The moon shone through the thin curtains and magnetically drew me to the window. I leant out, feeling the soft dew of the sultry night on my hot face. Cascading from the fountain, the water played with the moonshadows; thousands of tiny diamonds showering into the still, black pond below. The stone child came to life, beckoning me, tempting me, enticing me out into her world, laughing. Who was that laughing? Even Bridie's gentle breathing could not stop me thinking I could hear things and as I turned back to bed, the coat flung over the back of the chair looked like a menacing old man, slumped in the corner of our room.

"Wake up, Ellie! It's eight o'clock! You'll have to wait forever for a shower if you don't get a move on." Bridie had her hair wrapped up in a towel and was rummaging for her make up.

"I'm not surprised you're up so early," I grumbled. "You passed out pretty much the moment we got back here last night."

"I was totally exhausted!" claimed Bridie. "That athletics training came to nothing compared to sailing all afternoon. Anyway, I think you were just jealous because we won the Treasure Hunt!"

"No, it wasn't that," I said, rubbing my eyes and trying to remember if yesterday evening had been a dream or a reality. "It's just that I had loads to talk about, but it'll wait. I'm going for a shower." I grabbed my towel and headed off to the bathrooms, where Bridie was right. I waited ages and ended up going down to breakfast with wet hair, looking a sight and dripping onto everybody's toast.

"Ellie, I know you spent the whole of yesterday with your head in the lake," Josh commented when he saw me, "but I thought you might have dried off by now!"

He joined us for breakfast and we chatted about the day's activities. The children in my dreams, the Green Lady, the fountain girl – they had all taken second place now in my top ten of worries. I was thinking of one thing and one thing only!

"I'm riding this morning."

"Yes. There's a group of six of you, I think. Rosie – she's the riding instructor – said they were not going to run a beginners class, as you are the only one who hasn't ridden before. But she thinks you'll be fine."

There goes my self-esteem! The look of complete despair on my face must have been obvious!

"Don't worry!" He continued. "She needs to keep most of the really quiet ponies for this afternoon when the children from Stoke Park are riding, but I'm sure she'll find you some retired racehorse which will do nicely!"

"Stoke Park?" asked Salim. "Where's that?"

I pushed the talk of retired racehorses to the back of my panic-stricken mind and answered. "It's a school for young kids with disabilities. My mum does some physiotherapy there once a week."

"That's right." said Josh. "There's a real range of disabilities. All the children have Moderate Learning Difficulties, but some have physical disabilities as well. The riding is always a big hit with them. It gives them real confidence."

"My brother likes it," said George, more to his bacon and eggs than any human being round the table.

"What?" I said

"Who?" questioned Bridie at the same time.

84

"I said, my brother likes the riding."

There was a bit of an awkward silence, but Josh moved the conversation on easily.

"Does he go to Stoke Park, then, your brother?"

"Yes!"

Another silence. I think the rest of us would have started talking about the weather, but Salim is not known for his tact.

"What's wrong with him?"

"That's not exactly the question," interrupted Josh. "It's not really a case of what is wrong with anyone....."

George continued to stare at his plate and shook his head slightly. "Don't worry, Salim.   The fact is that there is plenty wrong with him. He has cerebral palsy – and he can't walk or talk properly. He's six" he added.

"That must be tough at home," commented Josh, quietly.

"Yes," said George and returned to his bacon and eggs.

Maybe that explains some things about George, I thought. It is funny how situations are never quite what they seem. How little we know about people. How little people probably know about me.

I was the only one of our group riding and I have to say, it was a lot more successful than the windsurfing. Gathering at the stables, I admit I was pretty terrified inside. The others all looked really confident and most of them had their own hats and riding gear. Rosie came out and asked which one of us was Ellie.

I went red. "Uh – that's me," Everyone was staring at me.

"OK," said Rosie. "Now, you're going to ride Trojan. Don't panic! He's not as violent as his name suggests. He's a super pony, very kind to beginners so you have nothing to worry about. But because the rest of the group have ridden before, I am going to stick with you and Sally – here's Sally coming cross the yard now – Sally will lead the rest."

The ponies were brought out one by one, and then Sally called out our names. Jo was first and she looked relaxed and happy, stroking the neck of a lovely 14 hand chestnut that stood stamping its foreleg on the cobbled yard. She checked the girth and then swung herself easily up into the saddle, where she just seemed to fit naturally. Like the girl in "Straight to the Top!" I thought to myself, a little jealously. The other girls followed on. Only Amanda had a bit of a struggle; she is quite small and fat (not being rude, but it's the truth) and she couldn't get her foot into the stirrup. Her pony, Eckles, started to go round in circles and Sally had to step in with an upturned milkcrate and give her bum a bit of a shove. Lastly, there was me. Rosie led Trojan out of the stables. He looked so kind, so wise. I approached him as though he was a wild elephant, but Rosie reassured me.

"Never show a horse that you are nervous. Come up to him and pat him. He won't bite!"

So I stood close to him and he nuzzled into my shoulder with his great, grand bay head.

"Don't be fooled!" called Jo from her chestnut, laughing. "He doesn't love you, just your polo mints!"

Rosie held him and explained how to mount, whilst I stood on the crate. It wasn't too difficult and soon I was sitting on Trojan whilst Rosie checked the length of the stirrup leathers. I loved it. From that very first moment, I loved it. I shifted slightly in the saddle, feeling my balance and leaned forward to pat Trojan on the neck.

"You're a natural," said Rosie, "I can see it already."

Although I am not usually boastful, she was right really. The windsurfing may have been a disaster, but riding just seemed to be something meant for me. Going round the indoor school to get used to our ponies, I could feel myself adjusting to Trojan's long stride. Even though I couldn't rise up and down when he trotted, I didn't feel too bad just bumping up and down. Towards the end of the ride, Rosie turned to me and suggested a short canter up the field.

"He'll just go alongside me, and he'll stop as soon as I do. Hold onto the pummel – that's the front bit of the saddle there."

"Let's go for it!" I was feeling full of adrenaline and happiness at the same time. We trotted for a few paces, I more or less let go of the reins with one hand and held onto the saddle and then I felt Trojan break into a rhythmic canter, like a rocking horse, and the wind was against my face and the sound of his hooves thudded against the grass and it felt like magic! I was laughing when we stopped at the gate – and yes - it was partly from relief!

"I don't think we're ever going to get you off Trojan," smiled Rosie.

Later at lunch, I bored them all to death.

"OK, OK!" said Javaad. "We get the idea and we will buy tickets to come to watch you at the Horse of the Year show. Now can we talk about something else?"

We did talk about something else, but I couldn't think about anything else. Partly about what fun it had been, partly day dreaming about how I could possibly get to go riding or even own a pony at home. But also remembering those ponies at the farm. Now I knew close up how well and shiny and happy the Highwood ponies looked, it made the farm ponies' condition even sadder. I had chatted to Rosie about them and asked her what we should do. She had said we should definitely get the RSPCA to check it out, especially in this hot weather. That was top of my list for when we got home, I thought, and I wouldn't do anything else until the ponies were saved. But there again, band rehearsals were pretty high up my list as well and I couldn't let Shareen, Liam and Andrew down. Which are more important, animals or people? I would have to do both.

I was right that walking was a bit of a problem after riding. I could hardly get up after lunch and Salim made plenty of not very funny comments about bow legs and Lewis contributed a joke about cowgirls as I struggled to leave the canteen looking even vaguely dignified. So I was pleased I had chosen music in the afternoon and I was also genuinely pleased to see George had chosen it too. There were only about seven of us and Josh was leading the session which was all about song writing. George and I paired up and after some discussion and warm up exercises we made our way out in to the garden to work as a pair – he was responsible for the melody and me for the lyrics. The plan was for us all to meet back after the break, share what we had done and even try to record some music if we were ready.

George and I were eager to get going. It gave us a great opportunity to try out some songs for the band. Oh, the band! Just the mention of it gave me butterflies: singing at school had been one thing; singing in the regional finals was going to be a whole new form of torture.

Sitting in the shade under one of the ancient beech trees, we experimented with various tunes whilst the bees provided a sort of backing hum and a woodpecker played percussion! I was happily engrossed in our task, until George changed the subject and said abruptly;

"You heard the children in the garden too, didn't you?"

I nodded, uncertain what to say next.

"Was that the first time you've, you've….well, heard or seen something like that?" he asked.

"Here, do you mean?"

"Here, anywhere…."

I paused and looked at him. He was picking bits of grass and chucking them up in the air, watching them float down again. "Well, no. Not really. I've seen things before, but I've never really told anyone. And then, yesterday, when we

88

arrived...I was on my own coming down the corridor and I saw, thought I saw, a lady."

George interrupted me. "Long dark hair? Sort of old fashioned green dress?"

I looked at him astonished. "Yes, just like that. She went into the forbidden room."

"I saw her too!" he said, totally seriously. "Going down the stairs, last night, after we had finished our hot chocolate. Everyone else had gone up to bed, but I realised I had left my inhaler for my asthma in my coat pocket, hanging up at the back door. I went past the bottom of your staircase, there she was. And then she was gone."

After a short silence, I asked him something I had been trying to fit together, like lost pieces of a jigsaw. "Do you think there is a connection, between seeing her and hearing the children in the garden?"

George shrugged his shoulders.

"And," I went on, "Why us? Why is it only you and me who've seen her, or heard the children? It was obvious Javaad didn't hear a thing."

"Troubled spirits," he said enigmatically. "Troubled spirits attract troubled spirits."

I looked at him and realised what a complicated person he was. This, with the ghosts, and that stuff about his younger brother – I wondered if I would ever feel I really knew him. Yet at the same time, I increasingly felt that I wanted to know him better, wanted to be friends. I turned over onto my back and lost myself amongst the miraculous maze of leaves and branches and sky, hung over my head like a painting on the ceiling of the world. George's phrase was playing on my mind: troubled spirits! Not just ourselves, but the B&B children, the ghostly lady, the voices we had heard ... the voices.....

I could hear something again! Only this time it was not the faint mystical sound of children laughing in a rose garden, but an urgent sharp shouting, from an adult.

"Alice! Alice!"

It sounded like a game of hide and seek, but not for fun.

"Do you think someone's lost a child?" I said to George. He put down the guitar and listened. More shouts, different voices broke the through the peace of the hot afternoon and then we could see a man walking towards us. He was quite out of breath and started talking urgently to us, almost before he was close enough to be heard.

"Sorry to disturb you, but have you seen a little girl running this way? She's about seven, long blonde hair?"

George and I shook our heads.

"Can we help look for her?" I asked.

He replied, but his eyes were still scanning the park as he spoke. "Well, that's kind of you to offer. We're only worried because she's from the Stoke Park group and she seems to have wandered off from the stables where they had been riding. She has some learning difficulties, so she shouldn't be wandering about on her own."

George jumped up. "I'll just put the guitar back in the music room," he said "then Ellie and I will help you look. I'm George Webber by the way – Tim Webber's older brother."

"I thought I recognised you" nodded the man. "I must have seen you at some Stoke Park fete or something. Well, you'll understand the problem then. If you see Alice, she isn't great with strangers, so if one of you just stays with her to keep an eye and the other comes to find one of us at the house. She won't speak to you – she can't talk, but she can hear, so just keep talking 'till we get there."

George and I ran back to the house and put the guitar in the music room. The others were all still scattered round the grounds, but Josh was in there, fiddling with a broken CD player. We explained what was going on. He immediately unplugged the keyboard. He joined the hunt as well. There was no time to lose.

So, we searched. We searched the woods, the lawns, the vegetable garden, the football pitch, the ropes course. Some of the adults headed down to the lake. All you could hear round the grounds were people calling "Alice! Alice" When we started, I think everyone assumed we'd find her in a few minutes. After all, how could a little girl go missing in a place like Highwood when there was a wall all the way round the outside of the grounds, and so many people looking inside the grounds?

But as the sun sank lower in the sky, I felt a rising sense of panic. How was she feeling, this little girl to whom the world was already so confusing, now that she was lost in a strange place? One of my strongest memories is of an early foster carer taking me to the school Christmas carol concert of one of the other children who she looked after. I didn't know the school, I didn't know the people and I remember thinking that I didn't know my carer well enough to know what her legs looked like. Legs are all you see in crowds when you are five.

More people had joined the search as they came back from activities. We went into the canteen to get a drink and a biscuit and went straight back out again. George was talking to me about his brother as we searched. About how all his parents' attention had to be given to Tim now. How he understood that, but how lonely it made him feel. He talked about the times he hated Tim because of his disability and what that meant for the family, about how tired his mum was all the time, about how his dad stayed late at the office because he couldn't cope. But on the other hand, he told me simply, he is my brother and I love him.

91

"I can't imagine how I would feel if anything happened to Tim," he said.

And we both stopped, paused, realising that the search had been going on for two hours. It would not be long before dusk wrapped shadows round the park. The swallows were winging their way back safely to their nests hidden under the eaves of the barns. But Alice had not returned. Everyone was running out of hope and explanations. The police were called.

Back at the main house the teacher from Stoke Park looked pale as he thanked us for looking, but added quietly, "I'm afraid there's not a lot more you can do."

"They've searched the annex and the house inside out," said Bridie who had returned from her second sailing lesson. "But it might be worth one more look. Let's split up."

We went our separate ways, Bridie downstairs, George in the boys' corridor and me upstairs on the girls landing. I looked in all the bedrooms, even under the duvets with their teddy bears from home and pyjamas stuffed hurriedly under pillows. I tried the handle of door marked Laundry, but it was locked. I looked in the bathrooms, pulling back the shower curtains and pushing open the loo doors. Nothing. Nothing. Nothing.

Back in my own bedroom I stared out of the window, hearing the calls from outside drift across the peaceful evening. Alice! Alice! Then I looked at the fountain with the stone child. It was as though she was holding me, hypnotising me. My stomach churned. The stone girl was pointing at me, past me.

Suddenly, I understood. I ran from the room, down the landing to the top of the stairs. There was no-one about. Breathing so loudly I could hear my heart beating, beating, I put my hand on the dusty handle and pushed on the door to the locked room. It swung open. As I knew in my heart it would. And there, tucked under an embroidered bedspread on a huge four poster bed, was a little blonde girl, her smiling round face surrounded by mountains of white lace pillows.

"Alice?" I said.

She nodded.

Taking a deep breath, I tried to stop and think. Not usually one of my greatest strengths, but I knew it was important not to terrify her, even though I was scared witless. I scanned the elegant, fresh bedroom quickly. There was no-one else there. Alice did not seem frightened. I couldn't even stop to think how she might have got in there. If I left her to get help, she might run off again. But if I stayed in that room, who knows what would happen. Would anyone ever find us, or would I too disappear off the face of the earth?

The door was only half closed behind me and I could hear voices coming down the landing. Who was it? I smiled at Alice, who smiled back and I edged towards the door. It was Bridie and George.

Wedging my foot between the door and the wall to stop it closing, I peered through the gap.

"Bridie!" I whispered, loudly. I didn't want to frighten Alice by shouting. "Bridie!"

"AAhh!" she screamed.

"Shut up!" I said angrily, and she was so surprised by the tone of my voice that she stopped screaming. "Listen, I've found Alice. She's in here, in the locked room. Don't ask me how or why, I've no idea. But I can't leave her and I don't exactly want to stay in here forever, so please go, find Josh or that teacher from Stoke Park as quick as you can."

For a split second, Bridie stood rooted to the ground, then she was gone. She understood the urgency. George looked at me and I realised from the expression on his face that I must have looked like a tormented spirit myself by that stage!

"Shall I come in? I may be able to help?"

Relieved, I opened the door. More confident than me, he just walked over to the vast bed and sat down on the edge. He smiled at Alice and took her hand.

"We've been looking for you, young lady," he said, sounding totally natural. And he carried on, as if he was telling a story. "First we looked in the tops of the trees, then we looked in the rabbit burrows, but the rabbits said, try the squirrels. So we asked the squirrels in the trees if they had seen you but they said no, try the bees in the flowerbeds. So we asked the bees in the flowerbeds and they said no, try the cows in the field, so we asked the cows in the field and they said, no......."

He was still going when we heard the sound of Josh and the teacher coming up the stairs. They came into the room looking flushed and the teacher held out his arms to Alice. She wriggled free from the covers and jumped into his hug. He sat on the bed, with Alice on his knee and asked her the million dollar question.

"Whatever are you doing in this bedroom?"

At first I thought she wasn't replying, but then I noticed that she was using sign language. I remembered he had said she wouldn't talk, but I guess he meant using words we could hear. She seemed to be chatting away, nineteen to the dozen, using her hands. It was frustrating not being able to follow what she was saying straight away, but I could tell from the teacher's face that he was very, very puzzled.

"Well, that's a fine story!" he laughed. He turned to Josh and said "Alice says that she wandered away from the stables towards the big house. She came inside and met a very nice lady in a long green dress who told her it was time for bed. The green lady led her upstairs to the bedroom and tucked her up in this lovely huge bed and kissed her goodnight. Here!" And as he kissed his finger and then pressed it to the little girl's forehead, she giggled. "When she woke up the green lady was gone, but she thought she ought to stay in bed, like a good girl until someone told her to get up. Any ideas who that might be, Josh?"

Josh stared at the teacher, then at Alice, then at us. He nodded.

"I know who it is," he said.

"So do we" said George.

To See Through Glass Darkly

Chapter Eight: A Secret History

The teacher from Stoke Park had scooped little Alice up into his arms and carried her off to bed. Her own bed! The police cars had turned off their blue flashing lights and headed off back up the drive. Josh signalled to me and George to stay put in the locked room.

"I'll be two minutes," he said. "Just sit here and wait for me to come back. I want to have a word with the two of you, so close the door and, please, don't invite anyone else into the room. I know I can trust you."

Josh left, and we stayed, sitting on this gigantic four poster bed. Our legs didn't even touch the floor.

"Did you ever read the Princess and the Pea, when you were little?" I asked George. "I can't even remember the whole story, something about this Princess who piles up thousands of mattresses and there's a pea under one of them...."

"Why?" he interrupted.

"Oh, George! Only you could ask that! How do I know why? Why did the Billy Goats Gruff want to get across the bridge, for that matter?"

"To get to the other side?" George managed to keep a dead straight face. He did have a sense of humour. It just took some getting used to.

"Anyway, I remember this book of Fairy Tales and there was a picture of a bed, just like this one, about twenty feet off the floor. Think what it would be like, sleeping in a bed like this, with a roof!" I gazed up at the heavy hanging crimson drapes at each corner and the velvet canopy, trimmed with thickly twined gold thread.

"Not to mention the fact that you would have to share the room with someone else," added George.

Someone else's room. There were no photos or books or pictures. None of the sort of little things which make a bedroom personal, but there was a definite sense of it being someone's room. The large gold mirror on the wall reflected the long curtains at the window, made of the same material as the bed, and held back in loops either side by the same gold braid. A pretty blue and white china bowl and jug stood on a small wooden dresser, next to a low chair. Everything was clean, freshly dusted and the small glass vase of roses on the mantelpiece ensured that the air was sweet. Roses! Would I ever breathe that scent again without remembering these secrets: secret rooms, secret gardens, secret spirits.

Now I thought about it, this was so strange, I shivered. I was not scared, exactly, but uncomfortable. Life felt as though everything had shifted slightly, and nothing was quite as it should be.

"That's what some people think ghosts are," explained George, when I told him how I felt. "Now that scientists have more theories on time and space, they think that there probably is another dimension and that time could possibly, sort of slip. And that would create ghosts, and deja vue."

"Deja who?" I asked, not being too hot on French at the best of times.

"Deja Vue. It means literally, 'Already Seen' and it's that weird feeling you get when you think to yourself, I've been here before, or All This Has Happened Before. You must have felt it."

"Yes" I said slowly, thinking back, "Yes, I have. Lots of times."

Just then, Josh came back in the room, making us jump. He was followed by the teacher from Stoke Park, who I now knew was Mr Hurst. Josh closed the door behind him and there were the four of us, in the locked room.

"Thanks for waiting," he said to me and George. I like adults like that, the ones who don't just assume you have to do what they say, the ones who thank you and respect you for the fact that you chose to do what they suggested.

"I know the three of you must have loads of questions and I don't necessarily have all the answers – well, hardly any of the answers, I suppose. I thought I could at least tell you the background to the story of this house. But – and this is a big BUT – I would much prefer it if you were able to keep it to yourselves. I don't want all the rest of your party," Josh said, turning to me and George, "getting hysterical and running around all night trying to get in here. I want this room to be left in peace."

"I understand," said George solemnly. I just nodded. Mr Hurst, who by this stage looked totally exhausted, just nodded as well.

"It's all a mystery to me," he said. "I mean Alice can't read, or write. She has never been in the front door of this place so she can never have seen the portrait of this, this what did you call her, Josh? Green Lady? She can't speak, either, so I think it's really unlikely anyone would have ever had a conversation with her about it. I don't believe in ghosts, but I'm really left with no other answer...."

Josh pulled up the old fashioned chair, embroidered silk with no arms, and sat down on it.

"They call this a nursing chair," he said. "Can you see why? If you are nursing a baby, there are no arms to get in the way. And there was a baby in this room once. And a mother who must have nursed her. Let me tell you their story.

There has been a house here for well over one thousand years. It's mentioned in the Domesday Book."

George's face lit up "I know, the record which William the Conqueror had drawn up of every house in every village in England in 1086. Was it called Highwood, then?"

"No," replied Josh "It's listed as Hogewood. Anyway, it was a big and famous estate and at the end of the fifteenth century, a very important family, headed by Lord and Lady Bickley were given it by the King."

"Bickley? But that's the name on the portrait!" I gasped.

"Well spotted, Ellie!" said Josh. "The lady in the portrait was Eleanor Bickley, only daughter of a later Lord Bickley. She was born in 1620 and grew up like any other rich young lady would have done. During the civil war, her parents were loyalists – do you know what I mean?"

George nodded, of course, but I shook my head. I know a lot about Vikings, Greeks and Romans, but not a lot about Kings and Queens of England. Apart from anything else, I missed a lot of school when I was younger. I was always moving school because it was a question of new carer, new school. Even when I stayed for any length of time, I didn't concentrate much. I had other things on my mind. Doing well at school is a bit of a new phenomenon for me!

"Well, don't worry," laughed Josh, "I didn't know too much until I took this job and realised that I was going to have to get to know the history of this place pretty quickly. George, can you explain?"

George's eyes wrinkled in concentration. "I think so. There was a civil war in England between Charles the First and Parliament. Parliament had Oliver Cromwell helping them, didn't they?"

Josh nodded.

"Well," continued George, looking more and more like a History Professor by the moment, "there were loads of battles and the whole thing ended up with Charles 1st losing and he was tried and hung in 1649."

"Exactly right. So let me tell you how Eleanor Bickley fits into this. As I said, her parents supported the King. The King made Oxford his headquarters for a while and that isn't too far from here, so maybe they thought they would keep on the right side of him. I don't know. But it seems Eleanor fell in love with one Sir Walter Wolferston, and he was on the other side. He supported Parliament against the king. They never had a chance to get married, even if they could have done, because he was killed at the Battle of Newbury in September, 1643."

"That's not too far from here either," added Mr Hurst, who, because of the lack of chairs, was sitting on the floor propped up against the wall.

"No. Its only about 30 miles. You can imagine the news reaching poor Eleanor here, at Highwood House. Perhaps some secret messenger galloped up that very driveway, to pass a note to a friendly servant. Or perhaps her father announced it over breakfast, pleased that the Kings troops had won. But the worse thing was that it turned out Eleanor was pregnant. It seems everyone knew who the father was and her parents must have been furious. The baby was born in March, the next year, 1644, here in this room. But there was even sadder news. There was something wrong with the baby. It's difficult to tell what, but historians who have studied the diaries and letters of the Bickley family say they suspect it was some form of cerebral palsy.

"Like Tim!" whispered George, now looking pale in the dying evening light.

Josh nodded. "Medical diagnosis was obviously different in those days. All we know is that Lord Bickley, Eleanor's father, wrote in his diary that the baby was "twisted in bone and short of breath". And in those days, with so little knowledge and their religious beliefs, the family assumed that the baby had been born like that as a punishment from

God, not only because Eleanor and Sir Walter were not married, but also because Sir Walter had gone against the King by supporting Parliament."

"Life must have been awful for Eleanor," I said, thinking of the poor isolated girl, pregnant and giving birth with everyone around her hating her - and her loved one, dead on the battlefield.

"Yes, and it was going to get worse," continued Josh. "There is no record of the child being christened in the family church. That's the church you can see just next door to the house, beyond the parkland. The records there go back hundreds of years. So either she was christened in the house secretly to avoid embarrassment, or never christened at all because they thought she was the devil's work. So we do not know her name. All we do know is that she was a girl and that she died when she was about five years old and was buried in the garden, presumably because someone thought she should not be laid to rest in the family vault in the church."

None of us said anything. We thought of the little disabled child, ill through no fault of her own or her mother's, buried at night at the bottom of the garden like some old, unloved pet. It was overwhelmingly sad.

"Her mother, Eleanor, only lived another four years herself. It is said in the diaries and letters that she hid herself away, again in this very room, and would not eat and would not receive visitors. She finally died in 1649, on January 30th, the same day that King Charles was beheaded for treason in London. In this household, neither side won much in the war."

Mr Hurst shook his head. "There are never winners in any war. Only losers."

"She died in here? On this bed?" asked George, looking around him at the white cotton sheets, lace pillowcases and sweet smelling lavender bags.

"Yes, we think so and we think the portrait was actually painted after her death," replied Josh. "But she did not rest. I don't know what I believe about after life and I certainly never believed in ghosts until I got this job, but it seems that ever since that time, her spirit has wandered the house and gardens at Highwood. There are endless accounts, in letters from guests, diary entries of members of the family, accounts written by governesses who worked here and fled and never came back. Right from 1700s up until now. Shall I go on?"

"Well, you can't stop now!" said Mr Hurst, looking just a bit grey in the face.

"OK. Now, in the late Victorian times, about 100 years ago, people were very interested in the paranormal and all that and some famous ghostbusters came here. Some accounts at the time were saying that the spirit was very angry, throwing things and causing disturbances in the house. So they suggested that this room should be locked and kept as a place just for Eleanor Bickley. Dusted and cleaned, sheets changed, and fresh flowers – they recommended all this – plus they advised that the little garden where the girl was supposed to be buried should be planted with beautiful flowers and then kept secret."

George and I looked at each other. That explained so much.

"You two know what I am talking about?" asked Josh

"We do." I said. I told Josh how we had ended up in the Rose Garden by mistake on the night of the treasure hunt, how beautiful and strange it was and how we had heard a child laughing before we left.

"Other people have said that," said Josh "although I have never heard it myself. Well, the Bickley family were besides themselves by this stage, so they followed all that advice and since then, it seems that the only times the Green Lady – as poor Eleanor is now known – the only time she is seen is when she appears to come in and out of this room – without opening the door of course, and going up and down the main stairs."

George and I were speechless, but Mr Hurst had more questions.

"So how come Highwood House is now a youth Centre?" he asked.

"Good question. The last Lord Bickley, who owned the house until 1960 something, was a very good man – and a very rich man. His own daughter had died tragically at a young age, in a climbing accident in Switzerland. He was devastated and he believed that Highwood had been a curse for a long time on his family, with many of the daughters dying prematurely. So, to make up for the way the family had treated Eleanor and her little girl all those centuries ago, he gave the house to the Youth Activities Organisation saying it should be used to help children grow up happy and loved. The only conditions he laid down were that the Rose Garden should be kept beautiful and peaceful for the dead child, and that this room should be kept locked, but looked after and loved - for Eleanor, the Green Lady."

It was dark outside now. The summer sun had dimmed behind the tall oaks in the park and the heavy gold mirror on the wall reflected a huge quiet moon rising slowly over the oak trees. The room felt quiet peaceful, I thought. There was no sense of Eleanor at that moment. Just a quietness and a seriousness, each one of us thinking our own thoughts. Maybe Mr Hurst was thinking about Alice and her meeting with the Green Lady – how we all thought it was so strange, but how she had obviously thought it was quite normal. Maybe Josh was thinking about all the children who have been to Highwood over the past years and left, just that bit happier, just that bit more loved, as Lord Bickley had wanted. Maybe George was thinking about his brother Tim and all the similarities between him and the little girl buried in the Rose Garden. And me? I had so many thoughts in my head, confused pictures of the refugee children playing in the backyard at the Bed & Breakfast, of the voice of the girl in the garden, of my birth mum, out there somewhere but without her daughter – without me.

"Are you alright, Ellie?" asked Josh quietly. I brushed the tears from my eyes and looked at him. He was a very kind man. I nodded.

"I'm fine," I said.

"I'll add one more thing," he said quietly. "Not many children who come to Highwood see her. But those that do, are usually children who are struggling with something themselves, or who have at least had to face unhappiness in the past. I don't know you two well, but I do know this. Whatever difficulties you have faced, or are facing, you are strong, wonderful, intelligent and kind young people and maybe that is why you are sensitive to the sadness faced by others."

Josh walked to the door.

"We need to leave now," he said, "and please remember what I said about not spreading hysteria around the group! Or if you do, you can be the ones doing night duty!"

His joke lifted the atmosphere and he opened the door and looked into the corridor.

"Everyone has just gone down for dinner," he said. "We need not lie, but we can say that Alice was found, safe and sound, tucked up in one of the beds. Is that OK with you, Mr Hurst?"

"Well, it's the truth, isn't it?" he replied and we all went down the oak staircase.

George and I left the two men, talking by the front door and made our way to the canteen.

"We'll just tell them we've been talking to Mr Hurst and Josh about Alice and the kids and my brother and stuff" said George. "You'll probably need to tell Bridie later, but I'm sure she won't have said anything to anyone. She's too sensible."

It seemed funny to hear George describing Bridie as sensible, sounding like my mother, but it was accurate. Bridie was much better than me at knowing when to keep her mouth shut and it was a huge relief for me to have someone to chat to about it all, otherwise I would have gone mad.

We got through supper having to answer only a few questions from Javaad and company. Actually, once the excitement of Alice being missing and then found was over, they were all far more excited about the disco that evening. The disco – I had almost forgotten! Luckily, there was about 45 minutes between the end of supper and the start of the party which meant we had time to shower, change and generally get my head together.

I did still have one question in my mind, though, so as we left the hall I paused briefly and knocked on Josh's office door. He was inside, leaning back on his chair at his desk, staring at the ceiling. He looked very, very tired. Maybe that was because he was on his own and didn't have to look super energetic and enthusiastic like he had to when we were all around. He jumped when I knocked.

"Sorry to disturb you," I said apologetically, "but I just had one very quick question."

"Fire away!" he replied.

"It's just that I was wondering. Do you think the kids with disabilities who come here to ride are more likely to get drawn in by the Green Lady, by Eleanor, you know because of the link with her baby and that stuff?"

"I'm not sure, Ellie," Josh said. "I think you may be right. But it's not going to be a problem for the future because Stoke Park will not be coming riding again after the end of this term."

"Why not?" I cried. "They love it! Just like I loved it this morning! Just because of what happened today? That's ridiculous!"

Josh waved his arm up and down. "Slow down, Ellie! Its nothing to do with today's events. It was decided last month. Lord Bickley may have left us the house, but he could not leave us much money. We need some very expensive safety equipment here to carry on doing riding for these kids – special lifts and harnesses – and they cost over £1000. Without the equipment, we can't get insurance. Without insurance, we can't have the riding. I'm afraid we just don't have the money, nor do Stoke Park."

"But there must be other ways of getting that money," I said. "The Government should pay, or a charity, or the National Lottery or something like that."

Josh shook his head. "We need money here for a lot of things," he said "and we have had grants from various charities, but it seems for the moment that this last £1000 is just one problem too far. Maybe something will turn up next year, but for now, we've had to cancel. It was the last thing we wanted to do, believe me."

And he turned back to his desk and I picked up the signal that he didn't want to discuss it further. I didn't know if George knew, or if Stoke Park and the kids knew for that matter, so I decided not to tell what Josh had just said, but inside it made me feel really, really angry. When I thought of all the things people did with £1000 and then the kids not being able to come riding each week, life seemed very unfair.

There are hard choices in life, aren't there? What would happen, for example, if I went home and suggested that we missed our family holiday this summer and gave the money to Highwood? Would I do that? Would I put my money where my mouth was, as the saying goes? Then I thought about school and about how the government had just spent £2000 on a new floor for the gym (I only know that because that is what the PE staff yelled at you every time you walk across it in your shoes!). Which do we need more? A new floor for our poxy gym, or a winch so that the little disabled kids can go riding? I know which I think is the more important. And then the other day, on the BBC news, I heard about some businessmen who earned over a million pounds – just as their bonus! What a crazy world! A million! And all that was needed here was £1000! But no choices are simple, are they? The world is so complicated. Which do you spend more on, for instance, helping old people have a decent end to their lives, helping little kids in England to go riding, or sending money abroad to help people who are starving to death?

One thing was clear in my thinking, though. There are many causes worth fighting for and I had just discovered one of them.

Chapter Nine: A Promise

"Ellie, tell me what's been going on. I could hardly keep my mouth shut at supper, but I could tell you didn't want to talk then," pleaded Bridie. We were lying on our beds, trying to summon up the strength to get ready for the disco.

So I told her the sad story of Eleanor, the Green Lady, her lover and her baby all those hundreds of years ago.

"And you believe it all? " she asked, quite seriously.

I nodded.

"And what about George? And Josh?" she added.

"George, yes" I said. "And Josh, yes as well. I think. Although maybe in a different way from me. I can't explain." I looked at Bridie. "And you? What do you think?"

"I just don't know," Bridie said, sitting up and crossing her legs on the bed. "I mean I haven't seen anything, like you have, so it's hard. But I can see how it could happen and I definitely wouldn't rule it out. You see, if I believe in God, and I do, then it's not so weird to believe in spirits and things, is it?"

"No, I suppose not. It's just I'm the other way round. I believe in the spirits and things, but can't quite work out the God thing!" – and we both laughed.

"Listen to us. Like a couple of old nuns. Ellie, we've got a disco to go to in ten minutes!"

We leaped into action. Never have two girls got ready for a night out so quickly, partly helped by the fact that we did not have to choose what to wear because we only had what we had packed in our cases. Bridie helped me with my hair and make up, because I am hopeless and, without sounding too boastful, we stood in front of the only full length mirror in the girl's bathrooms and awarded ourselves at least eight out of ten! The gong went – it didn't make us jump any longer – and we charged off to Hayley's room to meet up with them.

"Strength in numbers!" screeched Rachel.

"We'll need it with Salim on the prowl," I warned them.

"What do you see in him, Bridie?" asked Hayley.

Bridie almost fell headlong down the stairs. "Me? See in Salim? You have never been so wrong! I think he's a creep. He just hangs out with Javaad and so tags along with me and Ellie."

"But I think Javaad is pretty fed up with him this week," I added.

Bridie continued the analysis – rather loudly as usual. "You could feel sorry for him if you thought about it long enough. I mean I don't think anyone likes him really...."

"SShh! He's right there!" giggled Rachel, pointing down the stairs and we all collapsed, bent double with hysterics! "Don't worry, Salim," she called, "we were just all talking about you!"

The disco was held in the cellar. We clattered down the steep stone steps to where the music was thumping, the bass beat bouncing off the stone walls. I wonder if anyone will ever dance to the music of Glass Darkly, I thought to myself a bit optimistically, and then felt a flutter of nerves as I remembered the regional finals. They would only be two weeks away when we got back from Highwood.

The cellar had quite good lighting, loads of soft drinks and crisps and snacks and you could put in requests. About half way through the evening, there was a karaoke spot and we got together in huge groups to belt out the usual favourites. The teachers were there, trying to jig away in a not so cool fashion. "Bless them for trying!" was Bridie's rather patronising comment! George was there, propping up the walls, but since as we now know, they had been standing for about one thousand years, I think they could have managed without him. Javaad was with a group of the boys on the genuine 1960s pinball machine they had down there, but Salim had broken free and was predictably hanging around Bridie trying to be witty. He kept trying to lure her outside, saying he had something "special to show her".

"That's what they all say! Can't you think of something a bit more original?" mocked Rachel above the sound of the music!

I ended up dancing with Lewis, who is really sweet but not really my type. (To be truthful, I don't really have a type. Since I have never been out with anyone, I could hardly know what my type is!) It was quite hideous when the music suddenly cut to this really slow number, but luckily he was as embarrassed as I was and we managed to sort of stumble away. I ended up opposite him again when we played "Tunnel of Love". Do you know that one? When all the girls make a tunnel, the boys run through and when the music stops you have to kiss whoever is in front of you! Very childish, totally dreadful and embarrassing, but admit it – great fun!

About fifteen minutes before the end, whilst everyone was just warming up for a blast of Hey Macharina, which I am far too uncoordinated to ever manage, I suddenly felt the urge to slip away and get some fresh air. I climbed up the cellar steps, passing a few girls on their way back from the loo - and Salim hanging around looking dumb.

"Hey Ellie, want to come outside with me?"

"Give it a break, Salim," I replied and turned out of the house, leaving him propping up the doorway.

The night air was wonderful. The lights from the bedrooms upstairs threw patterns onto the lawn. I looked up and worked out that the locked room must be the third window to the left. It was dark. I turned my back on the house and walked across the lawn, to the fountain. Dipping

111

my hands under the cool water pouring from the jug in the stone girl's hands, I splashed it over my hot face and looked up at the statue: Which of the ill-fated Bickley daughters did this statue commemorate, I wondered. Or was this a statue of the original little girl? It had no date on it. My mind turned to Eleanor and, as if drawn by a desire I did not even know I had, I found myself walking towards the rose garden. I crept carefully between the rows in the kitchen garden and then slipped through the gap in the hedge which we had discovered during the treasure hunt on Monday evening. Yesterday evening. Had it only been 24 hours? I couldn't believe it. I stepped into the garden and sat on one of the little stone steps.

It was as if the night had swept through the grounds in a dark cloak and gathered up all the rose perfume and thrown it into the sky, so that the whole garden was filled, from brown earth to the starry skies with the scent of summer. The pale roses shone in the moonlight and the tall yew hedges cut out the lights from the house, making this a world all of its own. I did not hear the child laughing and I did not see the Green Lady, but I sensed them there, waiting for something from me. The clouds moved over the moon and the garden suddenly seemed dark and black and I shivered. For the first time, I was scared. As my mind was struggling against the panic, groping like a stranger lost in the mist, I heard my name being called. It sounded distant. It sounded angry. There was a sense of panic filling the garden.

"Ellie! Ellie!"

"What is it?" I called out, but my voice was swallowed by the still black pond and thick yew hedge. I was on my own out here. Then I doubted what I had heard. Was it Ellie someone was shouting, or was it Eleanor? Was it me they wanted, or her?

Ellie. Eleanor. How strange that we should share a name: that she lost a daughter and I lost a mother; that we should meet here, at Highwood. I understood now there was a link between this history and my history, my dreams. What was it? And suddenly, from deep down inside myself, I understood what she wanted, what the children in my dreams wanted. A shaft of moonlight broke free from the drifting clouds and it was as if the garden breathed again. I answered their request.

"I will raise the money," I promised them. "I will make sure that Highwood gets £1000 so no children, no sad or homeless or poor or disabled children are ever stopped from coming here. Then you can rest in peace."

I said it out loud, both for them and for myself, to make the promise stronger. And this time, it felt as though my voice was heard, quiet but clear in the waiting garden. Was there going to be an answer? An owl swept low over the yew hedge and silently on towards the barns. There was no answer, except deep inside myself I knew I had promised the right thing.

Standing up, I felt for the first time the night chill on my bare, sunburned shoulders and heard the crunch of my shoes on the gravel. It was time to go. I squeezed back through the hedges and walked towards the house, to rejoin the end of the disco.

Strangely, the first thing I heard was not the music, but a deafening jangle of an alarm and Hayley shouting at me.

"Ellie, over here – everyone's been looking for you!"

Then I heard another, much louder, much angrier voice interrupting her. It was Ms Midler and she did not sound happy.

"Ellie Long! Thank you for bothering to turn up. You have kept everyone out here for ages. Now, I don't want to delay things any longer, so I'll talk to you individually later."

Now, while this little rant was taking place, I was staring speechless at the scene in front of me. The entire Canterton Highwood Group was standing in straight lines on the front lawn, dressed in their disco stuff but looking like some bizarre teenage army! Flashing lights – and not from the dancefloor in the cellar – were bouncing from the alarm boxes on the side of the old stone walls onto the shadow patterned drive, making everything alternately either blue from the alarms or silver from the moonshine.

I had no idea what was going on, except I had this strong sense that I was in trouble.

"Look, I know it's out of bounds and all that, but you can ask Josh, it's because of the Green Lady and the problems with the money, so I just felt I wanted to sit there, where the girl is buried....."

Ms Midler was staring at me as though as I was mad, or drunk or high or something.

"When the all clear is given, you will go straight to the meeting room, please. I don't want to hear any more of your ridiculous ramblings. You are the last person I would have thought would go missing at a time like this. Now, go and take your place in the registration line and we will try for one last time to see if everybody is present."

It seemed that I hadn't been the only one missing when the fire alarm went off. Bridie caught me up to speed, whispering as we waited for the teachers and Highwood staff to tell us it was safe to go back in. Apparently the alarm had gone off, everyone had left through the fire exits, but loads of people were missing when they called the register – including me!

"She went mental!" laughed Bridie, "rampaging up and down with her clipboard! Didn't you hear us calling?"

Before I could answer Bridie, we were given permission to go back in the building and there was a raucous cheer, which only served to infuriate Ms Midler even more. They had agreed to extend the disco finishing time by half an hour to make up for the time lost on the fire drill, but it seemed that I would not be joining in the last song. I had been directed to the meeting room instead.

This was sounding more and more unfair, to me. I had helped find Alice, as a result of that I had been told the story of the Green Lady by the Youth Leader of the place, and as a result of that I had sat in a Rose Garden for five minutes at the end of a disco. How bad can that be? I stomped through the hall and slumped on a plastic chair at the end of a long line. Salim, predictably, had been having a cigarette with a couple of other boys somewhere beyond the beech trees. Mya and Oliver had been somewhere together – who knows where, except apparently it had taken them a long time to come back for the fire drill! A few of the others had apparently got bored with the disco and had gone off to mess around on the ropes course – in the dark! Obviously, nobody had expected there to be a register called at ten o'clock!

"Ellie, perhaps it would be a good idea if I talked to you next. Come on in. Lewis, I think you can go back upstairs, but please go straight to your room and go to bed. I don't want to see you again until the morning."

I followed her into the office and sat down on a red plastic chair.

"Now, where were you and who were you with?" she asked.

What was she talking about? My face must have mirrored my total incredulity, because she spoke quite crossly.

"Don't do the whole innocent thing with me, Ellie. You are all in enough trouble as it is. I have been taking residential trips for ages and I have never had to deal with everyone going missing during the disco. I don't mind telling you I feel very angry and, well if I am honest, sort of let down. Let down by you lot. So please don't waste my time with the whole "I wasn't doing anything wrong" story: you must have been miles away not to hear the fire alarm."

Well, I was miles away in one sense. In a totally different world. But I was hardly going to start trying to explain that to an overwrought PE teacher in the middle of the night!

"You can ask Josh. He'd understand. We talked for a long time earlier today, about history and ghosts and kids and loads of stuff. He told me a story about the Rose Garden. You know, the one that is out of bounds, and I know it was wrong, but I really felt I wanted to see it. So I slipped away and went there, just to sit, on my own for a bit. I know I'm not allowed in there, but I promise you, Ms Midler, that is the worst thing I have done this evening."

I could see from her face that she was relaxing and she went on and said something about fire regulations and how if it had been a real fire, people would have had to risk their life trying to find me in the building. I could see her point. Just as I was about to leave, there was a brief knock on the door and Josh came in. He winked at me, which was funny, but I don't think Ms Midler saw. She told me I could go, but I had just one question I wanted to ask.

"If it wasn't a practice and it wasn't a fire, then what set the alarm off?" I asked.

Ms Midler looked at Josh. "I don't think we know at this stage, do we Josh?"

Josh looked at me. "It seems some things got smashed and that set off the sensors in the different parts of the building," he said, but then continued quickly, "I don't mean anyone from Canterton broke them. They just, sort of, fell."

I frowned as I tried to read the expression on his face: it was as if he was trying to hint at something, but didn't want to go into details.

"Anyway, everyone's fine now, so that's the main thing." he finished, a bit too cheerily.

So, no longer particularly fussed by Ms Midler's tantrum, but intrigued by what Josh had said, I left the room and realised that the disco had just finished. Bridie commiserated with me as walked back along the corridor with everyone heading to bed. We had to step aside because one of the staff was on their hands and knees at the bottom of the big staircase, sweeping some broken glass into a dustpan. I looked up and realised with a shudder that it was from the portrait of Eleanor: the glass had shattered and it was as if she was staring down at us now, with no barriers, no façade. So that was what had triggered the alarm. And it must have been at exactly the same time as my experience in the rose garden.

Bridie woke me up the next morning, drawing the curtains. As I rolled over, I caught sight of her face and she was smiling.

"So what time do you call this?" she said, in a particularly annoying voice.

"You sound more and more like my mother." I shifted and sat up in bed. It was very bright and the sun already felt hot coming through the big window. I looked out. Everyone else was outside in the park, lining up. "What on earth is going on out there?"

"Everyone's getting ready for the activities," replied Bridie. "We're doing the high ropes course, remember? Its 9.30!"

And what was my most urgent thought? You're right! I'd missed breakfast. Bridie is a mind reader. Well, at least when it comes to me. That's what close friendship does, I suppose.

"Don't stress!" she laughed. "They've kept you some bacon and toast! Josh spoke to Ms Midler and backed up your story and they agreed you were probably pretty knackered and should be left to your beauty sleep. I felt like telling them that no amount of sleep would solve that problem…..Ms Midler said she'd speak to you this morning."

I pretended to thump Bridie, but then said, a bit more seriously. "Well you can tell your best friend Ms Jump to Conclusions Midler that I don't want to talk about last night ever again. I just want to get on with enjoying my last morning here."

Yes, we only had a few hours left at Highwood – and we wanted to make the most of them, so I put all thoughts of spirits and fire alarms out of my mind and we hurtled down the stairs to join the others, grabbing bacon and toast on the way.

"There are some limited benefits to being your friend," mumbled Bridie, incoherent with half a bacon buttie in her mouth. "At least I get two breakfasts! But there again, there was one portion left over."

"Why?" I mumbled with my mouthful.

Bridie raised her eyebrows as she replied. "Salim's!" she said. "He was packed off home first thing this morning."

"He what?" I exclaimed.

Bridie filled me in. It turned out that his exciting little invitations to lure us out of the disco were based on the fact that he had smuggled a bottle of vodka into Highwood and of course, he had been caught out when he lurched up to the fire alarm reeking of booze.

"What an idiot!" was my charitable response.

"Why does he need to show off all the time?" wondered Bridie. "It's not as if anyone was impressed. He couldn't even find anyone to drink it with him."

I was feeling heartless. "Well, at least we got his bacon!"

Outside, we joined up with Javaad and Lewis, and George – who had taken Salim's place on the ropes course. Lewis came up and gave me a big hug, which was a bit of a shock, but kind all the same. Josh came over, with a couple of hard hats in his hand.

"Nice of you two ladies to get out of bed and join us!" he laughed. "You've got some catching up to do, so get the gear on and come and join the briefing."

It was so like Josh, not to make a big deal out of the whole thing, not to make embarrassing comments. He was the sort of adult who made you feel special and cared about, without having to say anything.

If the ghosts and the hunt for Alice and the fire alarm hadn't been enough to bring us all together and strengthen our friendship, then the High Ropes course certainly was. High meant High. Very High. And Course meant getting from one end to the other without killing yourself. It was just what we all needed. A bit of the right sort of adrenaline, and by the time we were all safely down on planet earth with our feet firmly stuck to the ground, everyone was shouting and laughing and comparing photos on our digital cameras.

"Look at Javaad's face on this one!" screamed Bridie and we all crowded round to admire a classic of Javaad looking like a cross between Frankenstein and a demented sloth, hanging upside down from a rope thirty feet above the ground, grinning!

"Plenty of revenge in here" smiled Javaad, patting his camera and then running off at top speed across the grounds, back to the house for lunch. Bridie and Lewis set off in hot pursuit, but George was too puffed to catch up and I just enjoyed wandering along. Josh followed, gathering up discarded jumpers and dropped watches.

"Josh?" I asked.

"Sounds ominous!" he said. "What now?"

"Would you mind if George and I said a quick goodbye to the ponies? I know the stables are out of bounds without an adult and I don't want to get into any more trouble..."

Josh said he was going that way and would wander over with us, which would solve the problem. As we walked, I shared my thoughts from the night before with both of them.

"I've been thinking," I started.

"Careful, it may hurt!" joked George.

I ignored him. "I've been thinking, we could hold a few fundraising events at school and try to raise some money to help Highwood buy the winch and equipment for the Stoke Park kids to come riding. You know, cake sales and non-uniform days. That sort of thing."

Josh stopped and turned round. "That would be brilliant!" he exclaimed. "Mind you, it's a lot of money, but every little helps. It would all build up and we might get there eventually. Thanks Ellie – that's a fantastic idea."

We reached the stables and Josh went over to one of the storage sheds to pack away some ropes and harnesses. George and I leant on the railings. He was silent for a while, then he said, "I know it sounds mean, but sometimes I think, oh God, not another thing for Tim, for Stoke Park. Even coming here, to get away and here it all is again as though there is no escape. No, don't interrupt. But then I thought, of course there is no escape. Tim is my brother. I wouldn't want to walk away from him." George looked straight at me. "Do you know, the band is the best thing that has happened to me at CCC. You have been so kind to me, because I know I

120

am not exactly cool. The least I can do is help you with your campaign to raise some money. I'm in!"

After a rowdy lunch, we cleared our rooms. I looked out of the window at the stone girl on the fountain and smiled to myself. I took a picture of her and resolved to keep it pinned up on my noticeboard above my desk in my room, close to the zoo photo. Somehow, they sort of went together. And it would act as a reminder of my pledge. We dragged our cases down the landing, past the locked door of the locked room. I paused. Inside me, deep inside myself, I passed a message on to Eleanor, the Green Lady. See you later. With good news. On down the stairs to the hall and past the portrait and then out onto the lawn, with just a glimpse of the Rose garden through the gap in the yew hedge. I can hardly believe it all happened, I thought, stepping onto the coach. But it is not over, either. And it will not be over until the ghosts can rest peacefully, safe in the knowledge that the children are happy.

Chapter Ten: The Trespasser

What do you think Mum said to me when she picked me up? Six words starting with Did. That's right.

"Did you have a good time?"

How are you meant to answer that when you've had the sort of the three days I'd just experienced? It is difficult with mothers, I think. Sometimes I feel that I would like to share everything with her. Even though she is only my adopted mother, only a year or so ago, she would say "Did you have a good time?" and you couldn't have stopped me. I used to love telling her all about my day at school, and whether or not I got a gold star or a house point, or even if I'd been in trouble. I didn't necessarily share the things deep down that were difficult, but day to day stuff – that was fun to have someone interested in that.

But things change and now I've started at CCC, I still want to tell her things, but something stops me. I'm not sure what. Is it that I think she isn't interested and is just pretending – that's really patronising and, as you have discovered, I hate being patronised. Or is it that she won't understand how I feel about things? Sometimes, it seems, it is just a question of timing. She will ask me something when I don't feel like talking; then other times I do feel like talking but she will be just going out to work, or shopping or something. An endless mismatch.

"Did you have a good time?"

"Yes, it was great."

"Well, what did you get up to?"

"The usual stuff."

"What sort of stuff is that then?" she laughed, but I knew it was a laugh that was only covering up her exasperation or sadness. I'm not sure which.

"What sort of stuff do you think?" I was really tired. Now that I had got off the coach, all the emotions and dramas of the past few days seemed to overwhelm me and I felt exhausted. So I was cross as well. The rumour mill hadn't seemed to have got news to her about Salim and his alcohol, otherwise that would have been another million questions. Poor Mum. She just turned up the radio a bit louder and we drove home listening to the news. More politicians rabbitting on about tax; more football scores; more celebrity "disasters". Why don't people ever talk about the things that really matter? Like the children from Stoke Park not being able to go riding; or the ponies at the farm starving to death?

The ponies! I had almost forgotten them. As soon as I had dumped my stuff in my bedroom, and ignoring Mum going on about putting my washing in the machine, I ran downstairs. Chris was not back from his school trip to France yet, so I couldn't ask him.

I was frantic. "Mum, did Chris remind you about the ponies?"

"No. Should he have done?" she replied. "And please bring down your washing."

"Mum, this is important!" I shouted. "I asked him to remind you about checking on the ponies. It's been really hot. He's so selfish. He never thinks of anyone but himself!"

Mum stared hard at me. "That's hardly fair. You were the one so concerned, but you didn't go and check on them yourself before you left. You were so busy with the band and packing. You can hardly blame Chris."

"You always stick up for him," I yelled, unnecessarily loudly, considering we were both in the kitchen, and even when I had stamped back upstairs to my room, ours was only a small house and it was hardly a million miles between my room and her ears. But the truth is like that, isn't it? It always hurts. I did feel guilty. And if someone had to draw a graph in Maths, plotting the relationship between my temper and my guilt, you would see a pretty straight line, zooming off the top of the scale! Like this!

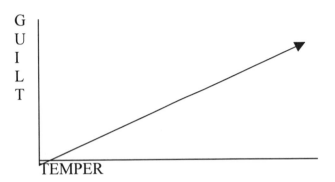

I took my washing downstairs in an attempt to make peace.

The next couple of days at school there was so much going on, Highwood seemed miles away. The band had to practice, for a start. The regional finals were creeping up fast and the competition was going to be tough. But equally, I really wanted to get going on fundraising for the children. And then there were the ponies....Bridie came round in the evening and we tried to get some ideas about raising money. We were sitting up in my room, brainstorming.

Bridie got another one of her big bits of paper and wrote Brainstorm in big flowery letters at the top and then sat and doodled.

Disco

I don't know if you've ever run a disco but it all seemed quite complicated the more we thought about it. We guessed we could have the school hall for free, but that isn't exactly what you call an exciting "venue". Then we would need someone to do the music, and the lights, and drinks......and even if half our year group turned up they wouldn't pay more than about £2 each so that only made £150 before we paid for anything.

1. Sponsored something or other

Sponsored what? We were too young to do anything really interesting like a parachute jump. Bridie's cousin had done a bungee jump for charity to help fund her gap year when she went to teach in Africa and raised quite a lot of money. But we would have to do something seriously dull like a sponsored walk, or a sponsored silence (impossible) or a sponsored swim (and as you know, me and water don't mix too well.) Bridie suggested a sponsored drown for me and said loads of people would pay to see me sink, which is probably true and not that funny. So I said she could do one of those sponsored shaves (Mr Bird did one at school, only I suppose it is OK for a man who is meant to be hairy.....).

2. Food

Now, I don't know about your school, but food is a sure winner at Canterton. When there was a big earthquake in Pakistan, all the Asian mums cooked delicious samosas and bajis and the kids sold them at lunchtimes. They made so much money that the nasty greedy money grubbing company which runs our school canteen and rips us off everyday started complaining that they were losing business! So, things like a cake sale, or selling ice creams at sports day seemed quite a good idea. If everyone in the school bought one thing to eat for 50p, we would make loads....So we put a tick in brackets next to the idea of food.

3. Non Uniform Day

Of course! It might have been the last thing that our slow brains got to, but it was the obvious answer. It took no effort, everybody always joined in. They only had to pay a pound each and – abracadabra - £1000.

"I can't believe we didn't think of that straight away!" said Bridie. "We must be getting really slow in our old age!"

"It's perfect," I agreed. "All we have to do is get permission – and they can hardly say no – print off some posters and go round the classes explaining."

"Or say something in Assembly," interrupted Bridie

"Exactly!" I continued. "And we should raise the money in no time!"

We were on a roll so we started working on the posters on my computer there and then and produced a couple of really great fliers explaining all about the riding and the special equipment. That problem was solved.

So, with the band on course, the fundraising sorted, that just left the ponies. Bridie is not known for her way with animals, nor is Javaad for that matter. I didn't want to walk round to the farm on my own, but I couldn't think who to ask to come with me. I wondered about asking George, but that would mean asking him round to my place which would be embarrassing. There were no more excuses. I had to go. Even if that meant on my own. After school, I dumped my bag and changed into my jeans and a tee shirt. It was a boiling hot day. The weather forecast had said that the heatwave was going to last at least another few days. I drank a huge glass of water and put on my trainers. The ground was so hard now I did not even have to wear boots to go through the woods. Rubbing suncream into my face and shoulders, which were a bit pink after Bridie and I had spent too long in the garden yesterday afternoon, I thought about how unbearable it must be for the ponies. And of course, I knew more about horses after Highwood where I had learned what it took to provide even a basic level of care: shelter, water, food.....three things which Mr Wilton's ponies certainly didn't have.

I went the long way round, just as we had with Mum and Dad a few weeks ago, so I could come into the yard the back way, not via the road. I didn't like the idea of having to walk past Mr Wilton's front door and have him stare at me, even if I was on a legal footpath. The bluebells weren't out any longer, but it was still beautiful in the wood. The trees shaded me from the glare of the white hot sun, I sat for a moment on the stile, feeling the cooler air against my skin and with my eyes closed, and I breathed deeply. Such peace, so sweet. A faint scent reminded me of the secret garden at Highwood and the children's voices. I opened my eyes and saw a wild rose climbing through the hedge. It was the smell of roses from the garden and the smell of lavender from the locked room. For a moment, everything in the whole world seemed connected and I felt myself spinning.

The shouts of some farm workers in the distance brought me back to earth and I climbed off the stile and out of the wood. Towards the farm. A group of cows were bunched together making the most of the shade in the corner of the field, and flies hung in great clouds above their heads. I trudged over the rutted track, where the mud had dried into hard, parched ridges and, hearing my heart beat a little faster, climbed over the fence into the yard. It was very quiet. A door banged somewhere in a barn and a dog barked, just once. There was a smell of petrol hanging in the hot air, with no breeze to take it away. I crept slowly through the yard until I could see the small paddock where the ponies were tethered. Nothing had changed. Nothing. Except that the ground was even harder; the flies were even thicker; the head collar looked even tighter. The little grey pony was hanging his head, just occasionally swishing his tail to chase off the insects. He didn't even seem to have the energy to stamp his hoof. Next to him, the slightly bigger bay was chewing at the wood on the fence. Flies were gathering around the sore behind his ear where the headcollar had rubbed. Their coats were dull and eyes half closed. How could I have forgotten them?

I edged my way slowly towards their enclosure, trying to keep half an eye out for the farmer. However angry I was, I did not want to tackle him on my own. Suddenly, my foot caught on a roll of barbed wire, half hidden in the weeds and rubbish in the yard. I fell forward and landed hard on an old piece of corrugated iron. The ponies jumped at the noise. Their heads pulled violently against the ropes which tied them down. Their eyes rolled wildly. My jeans were ripped at the knee and there was blood on my hands.

"That's the problem with trespassing," said a rough, loud voice, very close.

I scrambled up, nettles stinging my bare arms. There, right in front of me, was a man – well a teenager. He was dressed in oil smeared overalls and his hands were black and stained. A baseball cap, the wrong way round, had "Me First" written across it and his smile seemed to match the slogan. He was laughing at me and enjoying my pain.

"I'm not trespassing," said a voice from somewhere. I couldn't believe it was my voice. Shut up, I told myself. Now is not the time to get involved in an argument with someone like him. Yes it is, said the other me. He's vile. Look at him. He must know about the ponies and he's done nothing.

"I'm not trespassing," the voice repeated. "I'm on a footpath."

"The footpath runs from that fence to that gate," snarled the boy, pointing. "And you're not on it." He had a heavy spanner in one hand which he started flicking with his other finger and thumb. My courage was draining fast, as if someone had pulled the plug on my pool of confidence.

"I just wanted to look at the ponies," I explained.

"Well you've seen them now, so get lost."

Now or never, I thought to myself. Preferably never. Bizarrely, a song which my mum used to hum around the house crept into my mind. The chorus went something like -

"If you ever get the chance
To sit out or to dance -
Just dance!"

Well this wasn't exactly dancing, but it was the same philosophy. Sit on the sidelines watching the world happen to someone else, or get involved! So it had to be now! He started walking away, but I called after him,

"They don't look very happy, do they?"

The man stopped. He turned round slowly and stared at me. There was something very, very familiar about his eyes, but I couldn't place it and the recognition stirred up in me anxiety and fear. Who did he remind me of?

"Have you asked them?" he said sarcastically.

"I just thought they might need some water," I muttered, nervously.

"Water! Now, here I am, working on a farm, for a man who has been a farmer all his life, and whose dad was a farmer before him, and it never occurred to any of us that an animal might want water. Thank you so much for your advice. Now get the hell out of here, before I get my gun."

There are limits to my madness and I had just reached them. I was determined not to run – even if I could have done, my leg was agony. So I picked my way over the iron sheet and the wire back onto the footpath and strode off towards the gate onto the road. Without looking back, I opened the gate, closed it behind me and then, deliberately and in the most insolent way I could think of, I turned round and faced back into the farmyard and stared at him. He could do nothing about that, I thought. The ponies had gone back to their lifeless sleep.

There was still something about him that I couldn't place. A turn of phrase. Expressions. The way his mouth snarled. Do you know when you are trying to remember a song or a name and it's on the tip of your tongue? Well, it was like that. Except that it was a person and whoever it was danced around the edge of my mind all the way home, mocking me.

Dad was just pulling into the drive when I got back. He looked worried when he saw the state of me, with ripped jeans and blood all over my hand and my knee. He only works in the hospital in the personnel department, but I often think he must have secretly wanted to be a doctor or something because he comes over all medical at times.

Once he had established that I had fallen on rusty old iron, he decided I needed a tetanus booster and was about to plonk me in the back of the car and head into town. Luckily mum, who is much more laid back about these things, got back just in time. She pointed out that I'd had to have an up to date tetanus before I went to Highwood and that a bit of antiseptic and a wash would be fine. While she rummaged in what is meant to be our first aid cupboard, (which is full of out of date cough medicine that never worked anyway and indigestion tablets for when dad gets stressed,) she listened to my account of the ponies and the man.

This was one of our talking times. I hadn't realised how shaken up I felt, so I was glad to chat. At last she agreed that we should phone the Horse Rescue Centre, so we looked up their number in the book and I dialled.

"Thank you for calling the Horse Rescue Centre," said an impersonal voice. "We are sorry but this office is now closed. Our hours are 10.00 – 4.00 Monday to Friday. In an emergency, please call 07970 7981444, or alternatively leave a message after the beep and someone will get back to you as soon as possible. Beep."

I stared into the receiver. My mind always goes blank when there is an answering machine and I felt so angry that we had at last phoned them and there was no-one there, I couldn't think what to say.

I put the phone down.

"We better call the emergency number," I said to Mum, but even before I said it I knew what she would reply. Not exactly an emergency.....can wait until Monday.....they've lived this long, another couple of days won't make ...... etc etc. And I was right.

So the ponies were left again.

I had been a bit worried that once we phoned the animal rescue people, then the farmer and that horrible man would know it was me and might come looking for me. But that, I thought not so bravely to myself, was a risk I would have to take. Besides, I reasoned to myself that night, on line to Bridie, he would probably never think that a little girl (as he had called me) would phone up. It could be anyone walking on the footpath. They would never know it was me. Bridie pointed out the weakness in my thinking.

"If you thought you recognised him then he might have recognised you!"

The next morning I walked into my classroom for registration. The room was already boiling. I don't know who designs schools, but it seems illogical that there are all these highly qualified architects in the world and schools are always either freezing cold or boiling hot. Sonia and Javaad were arguing about whether it was better with the blinds up or down and Sean, who was completely barmy at the best of times and who seemed to have deteriorated markedly in the hot weather, was standing in the corner pouring water over his head.

"Mad dogs and Englishmen go out in the midday sun!" yelled Hayley at Sean, good naturedly.

"And trespassers," said Toni.

Hayley wrinkled up her nose at Toni. "What are you on about?"

"And trespassers," repeated Toni. "In the midday sun. They go out and snoop round other people's farms." She was staring at me, chewing gum and staring.

It was that stare. That was who the man reminded me of. He reminded me of Toni. Something about the way their eyes are close together and narrow. Something about the hatred you feel when they are around. Something about the sneer which curled their lips.

"What are you staring at?" I asked, although of course, I knew the answer to my own question perfectly well. Somehow there was a connection between Toni – the girl at school who I hated the most, mistrusted the most and had once feared the most – and that man.

"A trespasser!" she said.

Javaad had come away from the blinds and sensed trouble. He stood by me and asked what was going on.

"What's going on is this," said Toni. "My cousin Fraser works at Mr Wilton's farm in little miss sunshine's wonderful country village. He does the machines and the tractors and stuff. And who should he find snooping around the yard, but yours truly, Ellie."

"I wasn't snooping, I was on a footpath and if your cousin could read he would probably know that means there is a legal right of way." OK. I was being really confrontational, but I wasn't going to let Toni scare me.

"And that gives you the right to comment on their animals does it?" she demanded.

"If I want to – yes. It's evil the way they look after their ponies. They've got no water, no shelter, nothing. The flies are all over the sores on their heads where the headcollars don't fit properly. "

By this time, several girls in my class had overheard and came over, backing me up.

"Someone should ring the animal cruelty people!" said Hayley.

Sonia joined in. "Yeah! How come your cousin thinks he has any right to abuse animals just because they can't shout back?"

Things were heating up nicely when Javaad warned me and I looked up to see Mr Bettle, our form tutor, coming down the corridor.

"I could hear you lot like a load of fishwives, screeching at each other, right from the staff room."

Sonia laughed. "Come on sir, that must be an exaggeration,"

"Alright, not quite that bad," he admitted. "But can you cut out this arguing. If you've got a problem, sit down and talk it over like the sensible mature human beings you are meant to be becoming. It's far too hot for quarrels, even at this hour of the day. Now, I need to take the register fast, and in silence, otherwise we'll be late for assembly."

Which was, ironically, all about human rights. What about animal rights, I thought. Whatever happened to them?

But Bridie saw it a different way.

"Look, Ellie, this is a perfect opportunity," she pleaded at breaktime. "All that stuff at Assembly about disability and access and human rights and all that. It's perfect timing for us to ask to see the Head about the non-uniform day. She couldn't say no. Not after just giving an assembly like that."

So I agreed. We collected the posters we had made from Bridie's locker and went up to the staffroom at lunchtime and banged on the door. It seemed like only yesterday that we had been up there trying to sort out the money for Bridie to come to Highwood. It was like the world had been turned upside down since then. This time the Head wasn't available, but our Head of Year came out instead. Still chewing on her exceptionally smelly egg mayonnaise sandwich, Ms Seddon listened to our request.

"I can't promise anything," she said, picking a bit of cress out from in between her teeth. "But I'll put it to the charity committee."

"But how long before they meet again?" I asked.

"I can't tell you exactly when, but it should be soon," she said with her own, very special brand of irritating smile. "Now the bell's about to go and you two need to go and be in your classrooms on time."

She really was a very small minded lady, I thought as we went down the stairs. And a small minded lady who smelled of egg throughout her afternoon biology lessons. It doesn't get much worse than that! And as I went downstairs, past the office, past the medical room I saw Liam's Mum.

And I said "Hello, Mrs Burnett!"

And she said, " Hello Ellie. I hope this isn't going to spoil the band."

Right. That meant about as much to me as it does to you now. Nothing. And I walked on by, my mind so full up with anger at the two people in the world I disliked the most (Toni and Ms Seddon) that I did not think twice about what she was

135

saying. It wasn't until later that I heard that something dreadful had happened. Liam had fallen downstairs and injured his hand. Liam, our guitarist.

That's not exactly what I heard: I heard that Liam had been pushed downstairs and injured his hand. Pushed by Nicki. Toni's older sister. Or at least, that's what people were saying.

Waiting. Life is full of waiting. I am sometimes convinced that adults make life unnecessarily complicated just so it looks like growing up has been worth it. I was waiting for news on the non-uniform day. Waiting for news from the Horse Rescue Centre who had said they would "look into it". Waiting for the x-ray on Liam's finger. Not to mention waiting for the truth to come out about how he ended up in a heap at the bottom of the music block stairs, with a smashed up hand.

Nothing to do but wait. Wait and see, as mum says.

That night, as I lay awake, too hot to sleep, everything felt in the balance. From this point on, I thought, life could go either way.

Chapter Eleven: The Truant

I can't stand waiting. It's just not in my nature. It's not particularly greed or anything like that. It's just that I want things to happen now. Actually not even now. I think if I had my way I would want them happen yesterday. Tomorrow to me is next year. Next year is next century. Something went seriously wrong with my biological clock when I was created. If I write away for something, I look in the post for the answer the next day. That's why the internet is great. Things happen immediately, at the click of a mouse. So all this waiting was like a slow nightmare for me. The three things in life I really cared about – the band, the ponies and the fundraising for Stoke Park – they were all "on hold". The Green Lady had waited four hundred years for answers, for peace of mind. I couldn't wait four hours.

Maybe it's something to do with the fact that I like to be in control of things. If I am waiting, its means I am like a puppet and other people are pulling the strings. Although I look a bit shy and reserved to anyone meeting me for the first time, that is not the real me. I do need to reclaim my life. When you have lived with social care deciding who your mum will be, where you will live, right down to what colour your duvet will be, then believe me, you want to make up your own mind. Do things for yourself.

But on this occasion, there was nothing I could do. I had rung the Horse Rescue Centre, but they had no updates yet. It would be a few days, they said. I had asked my form tutor about the non-uniform day, but he didn't know anything about it and said he was sure Mrs Egg Mayonnaise Seddon would get back to us as soon as she had an answer. I had rung Liam's mum, e-mailed George and Andrew, texted Shareen – but there was no news on Liam's hand. He had stayed in hospital overnight until a surgeon could look at it and see if it needed an operation.

I had, however, found out what had happened to Liam's hand. It turned out that he had been coming down the stairs from the Art Rooms, just before lunch, when the people behind him fell forward, pushing into him and making him fall down the stairs. He had landed awkwardly and other Year 9s had said that his hand looked really horrible, all bent and the wrong way round. When they had called Matron, she had made him sit, propped up against the wall with a blanket for ten minutes before walking slowly over to the medical room where his mum could collect him and take him to casualty.

"Broken bones often cause sickness and shock." That's what matron had said.

Shareen said that everyone in Year 9 was discussing what had happened. Most of them seemed to think that Nicki had pushed Rhys, who had lurched forward, pushing into Liam. He couldn't help barging into him. The question was - as a "who dunnit" programme would say – did he fall or was he pushed? It seemed very convenient that Nicki and Toni's main rivals to the regional finals of the Battle of the Bands could now be without a guitarist. But equally, there was no way of proving that and Shareen thought that Nicki wasn't that spiteful. Not when she was on her own. But perhaps she wasn't acting on her own. Perhaps the others put her up to it. Certainly, Toni, Nicki, Dave and the rest of their band had all been seen, standing at the gates after school, laughing about Liam's "bad luck".

The evening dragged. I sat at my desk in my room with the window open, trying to get some homework done. It was far too hot to do anything and the numbers in my maths book jumped all over the page like grasshoppers. Chris was back from France looking tanned with his clothes smelling of smoke. Mum and Dad sat out in the garden, having a drink and enjoying the cool evening. The clock crawled round until I finally fell asleep, dreaming about broken fingers and people going to school wearing weird riding costumes and coming into my class where I was sitting next to the girl in the wheelchair who played in the yard at the back of the B&B. During the day and now at night as well, I felt as though my life was unravelling.

As I got off the school bus the next morning, I had to walk past Toni and Nicki on their way into the canteen where they hung out before the bell went.

"Really sorry about Liam, what will Glass Darkly do now they haven't got a guitarist?" Toni made no attempt to disguise the gloating tone of her voice.

I walked on by silently, rigid with anger, but soon caught up with Shareen on the picnic benches outside the technology block. George joined us, and then Adrian as well.

"Well…." said Adrian. "Don't keep us waiting."

Shareen fiddled with the straps on her school bag. "It's not good news. Liam called me late last night. He has broken two fingers on his left hand and strained the tendons round his thumb, or something. Anyway, his hand's in a sort of splint thing and its pretty painful…"

"And he can't play the guitar," finished Adrian.

"And he can't play the guitar."

Adrian got up and kicked the picnic table hard. Then he kicked it again. He was so angry, the whites of his knuckles showed as he thumped his fist down on the wood.

"This band, Glass Darkly, do you know? It was the best thing for me. The best thing that had happened to me. And now it's over. If I lay my hands on that tramp Nicki and her pathetic little group of losers, I'll make sure they never take part in anything, ever again. Ever."

I remembered George's words to me at Highwood. The same. "The band is the best thing that has ever happened to me" he had said. All of us, for whatever reason, had found so much fun and hope and confidence through Glass Darkly. And intentionally or not, Nicki and Toni and Dave and whoever else from Looking Black had destroyed all that.

I looked at Shareen. Even she had tears in her eyes. She was always so strong. The bell rang and there seemed nothing else to say. As we got up, I caught Adrian by the arm.

"Adrian. Don't do anything stupid. Please. If you go and get excluded, they'll have just won."

"Ellie – thanks," said Adrian. "But it's not that simple."

I watched him walk off towards the Year 9 form rooms in the History Block. Despite the heat, he had pulled his hood up over his head and his shoulders were hunched. He looked so alone. I hugged Shareen and then George and I walked off towards our form rooms.

"I'm going this way," said George suddenly. "Can you tell someone in my form that I'm here? Just say I'm in the music block then I won't get a late detention."

"Shall I come with you?" I asked.

"No. You go on and register. I'll meet up with you here at break I think it's worth talking to Ms Hensome," and George headed off to the Music Rooms.

Personally, I couldn't see what Ms Hensome could do about it. Even though she was magical as a music teacher, I'm sure she didn't have the power to heal broken bones. It was over and we had to accept it. You can imagine I was already feeling pretty down by the time I got to the form rooms and then, there was Bridie talking to our Head of Year. The Egg Mayonnaise teacher, dressed that day in a striking little purple suit with her bare, white legs sticking out at the bottom like loaves of bread. Bridie did not look happy. I could hear her voice as I pushed open the doors into the corridor.

"But that's stupid," she was complaining.

"There's nothing stupid about it!" said the Head of Year. "Ah, there's Ellie. Perhaps you can explain to her. I have to go to talk to Year 10 Assembly about Duke of Edinburgh awards." And she strode away, her hideous sensible shoes clicking up the corridor like a prison officer.

"What was all that about?" I asked Bridie.

"That was her saying that we couldn't hold a non-uniform day for the Stoke Park Kids."

"You've got to be joking?" I exclaimed, hardly able to believe what I was hearing. "Why not? That's ridiculous."

Bridie agreed. "I know," she said. "But apparently – " and here she started imitating the whining voice of Ms Hd Yr, "the school only approves three non-uniform days a year and the one for this term has already been allocated to Fish for Life."

"But why can't we have another one? People would pay to wear their own stuff on another day this term?" I persisted.

"Do you think I didn't say that?" grumbled Bridie. "But I can tell you, she's not going to budge. I'm not sure she even talked to the Head or the Charity Committee. She's such a kill joy."

"She's not just a kill joy. She only likes things that she's organised herself, she's a little power freak," I said vindictively.

It was a big disappointment. To be truthful, as Mum explained later, I can see that the school had a point. It probably did have to limit the number of non-uniform days and the school Charity Committee (voted for by the pupils) had agreed on the three top causes to benefit. All I could think was that we were going to have to go back to bake sales and sponsored walks. It just didn't seem fair, at that time, standing outside the form room with all my plans and hopes and dreams falling around my feet. To me, the whole school system seemed petty and unfair. The people who tried to make good stuff happen were just squashed; the people who succeeded in making bad stuff happen – like Nicki and Toni - they walked away laughing.

"I'm going!" I said.

"Going? Going where?" called Bridie, as I swung through the doors into the playground.

"Just going," I repeated and walked. I guess Bridie was just left standing there, gawping after me. All I knew in my head was that I couldn't spend the day in school. With tears streaming down my face, I walked. I found myself going out through the gates and onto the main road. I turned right down the hill towards town. All around me people were going about their daily routines. People driving to work, mums with toddlers in pushchairs on their way to day care or nurseries, lollipop ladies packing up and making their way home. I didn't really know where I was going, but after a few minutes, it struck me that I couldn't just walk into town. I'd be seen. It was so strange, just to have done it; to have left school. High, low, light-headed, depressed – it was as though I was on some sort of emotional roundabout, spinning and spinning. I turned off into the park and made my way past the swings and the slide to a bench, slightly hidden from the main path.

Watching the little kids being pushed on the baby swing – you know, the one with the bars across the front – part of me longed to be little again. Not my little. Not the little of care homes and placement meetings. But the little I imagined everyone else had. Little on the swing, little having your knees kissed better when you fell over, little, when the adults managed everything and tucked you up in bed at night and tomorrow was another day. I wanted to be grown up and powerful and small and invisible all at the same time. But that was not possible, that was not a reality. The reality was me, sitting on the bench, bunking off school whilst all my friends were in French and the teacher was asking where I was. Bridie would have covered up for me for one lesson, but she couldn't do that all day.

I didn't know what to do. I would feel stupid going back into school. But I was not sure I could spend all day hanging around town. Someone would see me. I looked at my mobile. It was only 9.20. Time inched its way through what would have been Period One. What if the police picked me up on one of their truancy sweeps? I could really do without that.

I picked up my school bag and heard my keys jangle. At least I could get home, I thought. I could probably fix some story up, if I went straight home. I was just thinking about leaving and catching the hourly bus up to our village when I noticed this man, leaning on the railings outside the public toilets looking at me.

"You all right love?" he called. "Can I help? You look a bit lost."

"I'm OK!" I called back. "I'm just going to get the bus. "

"Do you need any money?" he asked. "I can give you a pound if you're stuck."

He looked quite friendly and quite ordinary. He was probably in his thirties, wearing jeans and a tee-shirt, with a packet of cigarettes tucked into his top pocket. I didn't know if I had any money or not in my pocket. Perhaps he really would give me a pound. I hesitated. But then there was just something about him that made me wake up, something about the way his sharp blue eyes were looking me up and down and the way he seemed to have sidled closer.

For goodness sake, Ellie, I thought to myself. How many lectures have you been to on not talking to strangers and on staying safe? And here you are, truanting in the park and getting ready to take money off some strange old bloke hanging around the toilets.

"Or I've got my car, if you want a lift," he added.

That was it. I came to my senses. I turned and ran. The pigeons fluttered up into the sky in front of me and even the spiteful geese made a hasty retreat into the litter filled pond. I didn't stop running until I got down to the main road. And I didn't look back. I had been that close, I thought. That close to becoming a statistic. It would have been so easy....so stupid.

The 353 bus was coming round the corner, stopping outside the charity shops opposite the war memorial and I jumped on. I rummaged in my bag and found a 50 P and two twenties. The driver let me off the other 10P and I stumbled to the back of the bus and slumped staring out of the window. As it turned up the hill, I turned to look back at the park: the man had gone. We passed the school, everyone in their lessons, the car park quiet; we passed the Canterton stores where the postman was just emptying the letterbox; we went on out of town, through the suburbs which sprawled like octopus tentacles reaching out from the body of the town into the fields and woods. Finally, it reached my stop. No-one else got off. I wandered down the quiet lane, got home and let myself in to the empty house where the dirty breakfast things piled up in the sink seemed surprised to see me. It was so weird, thinking that I had just left school. That I had come so close to disaster in the park. That people would be wondering where I was and maybe ringing mum....oh my goodness! They would ring mum. I had to get to her first.

I sat on the bottom of the stairs and called her work.

"Could I speak to Mrs Long? It's her daughter," I said to the receptionist. Mum wouldn't panic. She would probably think I needed a lift, or was going out or one of the other hundred reasons I occasionally called her from my mobile at breaktime. It was now breaktime in that other world a million miles away – school.

"Hello darling. What's going on?" she asked. Thank goodness. I thought. I could tell from her voice that no-one had got to her first.

"Oh Mum. I just thought I should let you know that I'm at home. I felt really sick at school but I couldn't find matron. So I did a bit of a stupid thing and just left and got the bus home."

She sounded just a little bit unconvinced. Funny how we forget that our parents might have ever been teenagers!

"So how are you feeling now?"

"Oh, I'm feeling better now I'm home," I said. Which was truthful after all! "Maybe it's just because it was so hot and I spent too long in the sun yesterday. Anyway, I wondered if you could ring them and tell them you know I'm at home and safe and all that. I'll just spend the rest of the day in my room, sleeping."

Silence.

"Yes. I'll do that. Now, keep cool and drink lots of water and I should be home around 3 ish today so I'll see you then. Oh, you could take some paracetemol and ring me if you need anything! Love you!"

I had escaped. There would be some fall out, because of "not following correct procedures", but I would have avoided the worst accusations of truancy. I had also avoided the worst nightmares of truancy – getting caught up in some hell with weirdos who hang around in the park, preying like vultures on kids who are out of school.

When I put the receiver down, I noticed the message button flashing. I pressed play and listened, not expecting anything much. It was from the RSPCA.

"This is a message for Mrs Long from Richard at the RSPCA. Thank you for alerting us to the condition of the two ponies at End Farm. We have been round to the premises and spoken to the owner and hope that he will now be able to put things in place to improve the living conditions of the horses. We are very grateful for your interest and do get back in touch with us if things don't get better."

What? They hadn't even taken the ponies to their rescue home? They had left them there, with that disgusting Fraser cousin of Toni's and Mr Wilton?

It was the last blow in an otherwise unbelievably dismal couple of hours. There was nothing left now of all my hopes of a few days ago. The band was finished – we had no guitarist. The Stoke Park kids were never going to get to go riding again – our fundraising ideas had been squashed. And the ponies; well the ponies were presumably still there, tied up and sweltering in the heat. Nothing would be healed. The Green Lady would still roam restlessly round Highwood, seeking peace for herself and her child, looking for justice for all the ill children in the world and not finding it. Our generation had let hers down. The Bed and Breakfast children in my dreams were right; I could never give them what they were asking for. It always looked as though there was so much progress in the world, but at that point, it just looked as though history repeated itself, again and again.

What was the point? What was the point in even trying to change things? I didn't know. I followed my own advice and went up to my room. I flung open the window to let the breeze in and lay on my bed staring at my noticeboard. Amongst the pictures were the new photos from Highwood which I had downloaded and printed out. The little stone girl from the fountain looked down on me. In the picture the water continued to pour, cool and refreshing from the jug into the sparkling fountain. Don't give up on us, she seemed to say. Don't give up on yourself.

Chapter Twelve: Back on Track

"Ellie! There's someone here to see you!"

What time was it? Was it the weekend? What was going on? I rolled over and looked at my clock. It was half past four! I stared at it for a moment before I remembered what had happened. Six hours earlier I had walked out of school. I sat up slowly, listening. What was going on downstairs?

"Ellie! Are you coming down?" That was Chris yelling up the stairs. I don't usually respond to his dictator tendencies, but I sat on the edge of the bed, rubbed my eyes and decided to go. I didn't know if mum was back and if she was, it was no bad thing to have Chris around as well. He did usually stick up for me if I was in trouble and vice versa. I caught sight of myself in the mirror at the top of the stairs, looking like an old hag with my hair frizzed and standing up on end, my eyes stuck together and half my face beetroot red where I'd been asleep for so long on such a hot afternoon. I could hear voices in the garden, so I went out and there, sitting round our garden table in the shade were Chris, Mum and George! George!

"George?" I said.

"George!" I repeated.

"I think we know his name by now, Ellie," laughed Mum. "Are you feeling better? You must have slept for ages and you were very hot when I came back."

Brilliant. I must have actually looked ill!

"Yeah – I don't feel sick at all now. I must have slept it off," I said, weakly and not daring to catch George's eye. "Did you contact school? I don't want to get into trouble" No! Not me!

"Don't worry! I spoke to Matron and apparently she had been in and out of her room all morning so you may have missed her. She said you really must check out with the office next time. You must realise what a nightmare it is when some children truant. Not that you'd do that."

Sometimes I couldn't quite read my mum's voice. Was there just a hint of a warning in that last sentence? I can see now that underlying all their confidence as parents, there must have always been worries: worries that adopted teenagers get into trouble, get excluded, play truant, break the law......Hopefully, I'm living proof that it can turn out OK – well, so far anyway!

She continued.

"There's a coke in the fridge. That will rehydrate you and I'm popping out for some shopping so I'll leave you to it. Nice to meet you George. I reckon that's the sign of a really good friend, to bicycle all the way out here on a day like this," and she was gone, taking Chris with her – despite his objections – to "help her carry the shopping."

As I went into the kitchen for the coke, I overheard her!

"You are jolly well coming with me and giving them some space. There's more to this coming home early business than meets the eye and I think it would only be kind to give the two of them some time together....."

Oh my goodness! What did she think was going on between me and George? How embarrassing! I peeped out of the kitchen window and reassured myself. George was in his own world as usual – he couldn't possibly have heard!

"It must have taken you ages to bike up here," I said, carrying the cans back out to the scorching garden. "You needn't have bothered. I'm fine really. I just wanted to get out of school. It was all too much this morning."

George finished his drink. "I know. I understand. Bridie told me what happened and we just sort of covered up for you until afternoon registration when Mr Bettle said that your mum had phoned and you had gone home ill."

"I don't recommend bunking off," I said. "It was really weird. Being out and about and knowing that in some ways I was free, but in other ways I was guilty and scared. And then this pervert tried to chat me up in the park and that really freaked me out, so I got the bus home."

George's face said it all. "What? You should phone the police."

"I can't, can I? Everyone would know then that I hadn't just felt ill and gone home."

"On your head be it!" said George in one of his strange old age pensioner type phrases. "If a little girl gets dragged away and you never reported him……"

"Oh shut up!" I cried and chucked the remains of the water in the bottle on the table over him. "You didn't come all the way here to give me a lecture on Stranger Danger. What went on the rest of the day?"

I could tell George had something to say, but he half smiled and began "Well, there was French and then Art. After break we had double Technology…."

I gave him my evil stare.

"OK, I give up," he continued. "I went to see Ms Hensome and she told me to come back at lunchtime. And when I got to the music school, do you know who was there? Steven McVeigh with Shareen! And Ms Hensome just said – George – meet your new guitarist!"

I guess I was just sitting there, in my frizzy hair and red face, gawping at him, because he added, "You look quite extra-terrestrial sometimes you know, Ellie. Apparently Ms Hensome rang the organisers of the competition, explained what happened to Liam and asked if Glass Darkly could use another guitarist from the school to fill in. They said no problem and Steve was thrilled. He had been gutted that Patched Up hadn't made the regionals. So! We're still in the competition and Looking Black had better watch out!"

151

"And what does Liam think?" I asked, because although I knew he would never grudge us going on without him, it must be difficult.

"He's going to join you and Shareen and do some vocals."

This was the best news! The band would be better than ever. Steve was a fantastic guitarist in Year 10. Maybe we would win and go on to the nationals?

"That's one out of three sorted then," I said and went on to explain to George that it hadn't just been the band that had got me down earlier in the day. It had been the fundraising ideas and the ponies as well. George is not exactly a great fan of four legged beasts, but we did sit chatting about the fundraising. He told me how his brother Tim had now had a letter from Stoke Park explaining that the riding would stop at the end of term and would not be continued in the Autumn. Tim had cried, he said, which was pretty unusual, he was used to disappointment and didn't cry easily. All the kids there had been very upset, and the parents were trying to petition the Local Education Authority for some money.

"They would do the fundraising themselves," said George "but they are in the middle of a huge appeal for a hydrotherapy pool, trying to raise £20,000..."

"It's not just as simple as the money," I said hesitantly. George and I hadn't spoken much about The Green Lady recently. It was as if we were almost embarrassed about it, as if somehow it seemed silly now, looking back on it.

"It is more than that," he agreed. "It's to do with putting things right, as well, isn't it?"

I nodded and he went on.

"Its weird, but I overheard Dad talking to one of the other parents of a kid at Stoke Park, and they were saying that the residential holiday for the older kids may have to be cancelled because they had had to close off the old part of the house. Something to do with Health and Safety. But

152

apparently, they weren't able to be more specific than that. So I couldn't help wondering...." He paused and looked at me, eyes crinkled up against the bright sunlight.

"Wondering if it was to do with her?" I said, for him.

"Yes. Does that seem mad? But you know, I was wondering if The Green Lady had become more restless? Josh said, didn't he, that in the past there had been things thrown and stuff like that. Poltergeist activity, it's called. It would be impossible to have little kids there if there really were things happening. Like that."

"And that really would be the end of Highwood....." I began, but I was interrupted.

"What's this about Highwood?" said Mum, coming in behind us carrying some bags of shopping.

I explained about George, his brother and the problems Stoke Park were having about riding at Highwood. It turns out mum knew about it, from her physiotherapy visits there.

"I didn't know you were trying to raise money, Ellie" she said. "Why didn't you ask me? I'd love to help you. You may not be able to do a non-uniform day and you may not be able to raise all the money in one go, but you could start by doing a bake sale and raise the money bit by bit."

There it is again. The waiting thing. I didn't want to raise the money bit by bit. I wanted to do it all in one go. Preferably NOW! But George is much more grown up than me and, predictably, he agreed with my Mum.

"If you think about it," he said, with calculator pound signs going round and round in his eyes like a cartoon, "if twenty of us brought in cakes or brownies which divided into 10, that would be 200 bits to sell. And at 50p each, that would mean we had raised £100 and we would only have to do that once a week until the end of term to have made half the money we need."

Only George could think like that. It wasn't so spectacular. It wasn't so dramatic or so easy for that matter. But they were right. If it would raise the money in the end, we should do it.

The next week was a strange mixture of cooking and rehearsing – and I know which one I prefer. I am really not designed to be, how does Mum call it, a "domestic Goddess". My first load of fairy cakes were less fairy and more goblin: deformed, ugly and inedible. On the other hand, at our first band session in Adrian's garage, we were good, really good!

We had all been a bit nervous I think. Shareen seemed a bit less confident than usual with Steve around. I suppose he was Year 10 and very good looking! Liam got over the disappointment of not being able to play the guitar and actually, he had a very good voice. It added something rich to the vocals to have a deeper voice coming in. We needed to play one more number in the regional finals and we experimented with various songs until we finally decided to work on one which Adrian and Liam had written some time ago. Ironically, it was called "No More Ghosts" and was actually about not letting the past get you down – but George and I had to laugh, although we wouldn't tell the others why. Somehow I didn't think it would improve our image with the Year 9s and 10s if we started telling ghost stories about Green Ladies and voices in the garden! We didn't even really mention it between ourselves. It seemed like another world, in more ways than one.

Adrian's dad and his partner came in to the garage to listen one night and were really impressed. Jenny (that was her name) offered to make us all pizzas, but I said I had to get home.

"What's the hurry?" asked Adrian, looking a bit disappointed.

I explained that we had the first of our charity bake sales the next day and that I needed to get home and do more cooking.

"What's it in aid of?" asked Steve.

So I told them all about the riding and the kids from Stoke Park and how children like George's brother would benefit. George looked down, kicking an old rusty nail around the garage floor and I remembered that he didn't usually share private information with many people. Just me. And that had taken a long time. The others noticed his silence and Jenny jumped in quickly:

"I've got time on my hands this evening. If I bake some millionaire's shortbread – you know with toffee and chocolate on top – and send it in tomorrow with Adrian? Would that help?"

"And I could do something," said Shareen. "Mum would probably help me make some Brownies or something. I'll bring them to your form room in the morning."

In fact, the next day, our formroom looked like the headquarters of an International Cake Conference! There was an incredible amount of food. And loads of people in my form said they hadn't really bothered to read the letter, but now they knew what was going on and what it was for, they would make stuff next week. The Egg Mayonnaise woman came in and started making stupid Head of Year noises about nut allergies, but we were rescued by Mr B who said we could make a huge notice on the computer warning people that all of the cakes could contain nuts. He said his daughter had a nut allergy so he knew how serious that could be, but she was typical in that she wouldn't want her allergy to stop something as successful as the bake sale. Funny how human teachers are, when you get them on their own!

We pretty much sold out at morning break and just had one table in the entrance hall, with a few leftovers, at lunchtime. Two of us were given permission to count the money in the lesson after lunch – which given it was Chemistry with the dreaded, sweaty Mr Gannick was a big break! In the end we tossed a coin and poor old Bridie lost. George of course had gone to lessons! He was still hard to grasp sometimes!

Javaad and I sat out on the benches under the tree, piling up the pound coins and bagging up the change.

"How much then?" asked Mrs Midler, on her way to the PE office.

"£97.55" I said. "That's pretty amazing considering our target was £100".

Mrs Midler got a purse out of her track suit trousers.

"Here you are then," she said. "45p and that should make £100!" and off she went.

Like I said, it's impossible to predict these teachers. One moment she's accusing me of unspecified evil doings during a fire alarm, two weeks later she's donating money to the fundraising and without even getting a brownie in return!

We chatted about the success at our band rehearsal that evening.

"I know its great and all that," I said, "but we have to do that ten times to raise the money. That means we won't make the total until at least half term in October."

So Steve suggested that the Band could contribute in some way, by doing a gig or a sponsored play. He told us about a previous school he'd been to in Yorkshire where they had done a 24 hour music marathon! 24 hours of non stop playing and singing.

"One thing you can say about Steve," laughed Shareen "He's got stamina!"

And there was something about the way she looked at him…..

Another week, another bake sale, another £100. Another week, another load of rehearsals – and then it was the morning of the regional finals. And it began and ended with a bang!

The heatwave ended at exactly 3.0'clock in the morning on the day of the finals. There had been rumbles of thunder on and off for the past week, and sometimes a few drops of rain. Javaad had been telling me how it was like being in Pakistan waiting for the monsoon. Everything builds up, hotter and hotter, like a pressure cooker until you think that something has to give otherwise the world will explode. The odd afternoon, the sky clouds over, the darkness leans down on the waiting earth and you look up, holding out your hands to feel the first, few, lonely drops of rain. Drops which are giant and slow and ponderous - then come to nothing. And then the rain clouds move on, like a crowd after a match, and the heat returns and you begin waiting for the rain all over again.

Tempers were beginning to fray. The newspapers reported a rise in the crime rate. Closer to home, over-heated teachers dolled out detentions in sweltering afternoon classrooms and nobody turned up and nobody bothered to chase you; year 11s fainted in their GCSEs in the gym and little kids screamed waiting for the bus, ripping off their sunhats and throwing them on the melting pavements. The hosepipe ban meant we couldn't cool off in the garden and the outdoor swimming pool in town was so crowded at weekends you practically had to book you own square inch of water in advance.

Dad told me that he had walked through the woods in the evening to cool off and back through Mr Wiltons' farm and there had been no sign of the ponies. It was hard to tell whether they had been moved somewhere nicer or whether he had just sold them for dogmeat. I wouldn't put it past him. I promised myself that once the regional finals were over, I would find out.

I stood on my bed, pretend microphone in my hand, and went through my part one more time before going to bed. There was one really high note in "No More Ghosts" which I was very nervous about. Just as I got to it, the lights flickered and went out as the thunder growled around outside. Now if that was in a film I would say it was pretty clichéd! I climbed into bed and lay there listening to the storm and watching the flashes some distance away unzip the sky. Despite being so excited and so terrified, I did fall asleep, but was woken up again at 3.0'clock by the most enormous crash of thunder which shook the house as if the Gods had seized it by the throat and shaken it in anger. I sat bolt upright and then crept to the window and opened the curtains. Great jagged tears of lightning were ripping the sky apart and the wind grew stronger, blowing my curtains over my desk and sending my pens and photos clattering onto the floor as if the spirits themselves were swirling round the house. It was exhilarating and when it began to rain, I simply couldn't resist it.

I tiptoed downstairs and let myself out of the back door. Feeling the drenched grass under my bare feet, I stood in the garden, my face up to the crackling sky - laughing in the rain, singing in the rain, breathing for the first time for weeks, spinning round and round like the carefree little child I had never been. I felt that everything and anything was possible and that the universe was there for the taking. Don't worry, Green Lady, I called silently from the depths of my heart to the wilds of the thunder driven storm, we will see this through.

Exhausted and soaked through, I left puddles on the kitchen floor as I went back upstairs. I pulled off my nightie and put on a tee-shirt, shut the window, drew the curtains and pulled the duvet up around my chin. I drifted slowly into sleep listening to the rain on the windowpane and feeling strong and safe and happy. No dreams disturbed me that night. I was sure it was going to be a good day.

All the members of Glass Darkly and Looking Black had been given the afternoon off school to get ready and then travel to Hampton for the competition. We had to be there by five at the latest because we were allowed a run through on stage before the actual competition began at 7.30 and it was at least one hours drive away. Adrian's dad was taking his van with all the instruments and equipment, as well as Adrian and Liam. Shareen was getting a lift with Steve (which she was clearly very excited about) so George and I had agreed to go together. George had seemed unwilling to be picked up at his place and it was impossible to pin him down to arrangements. In the end, the phone had gone at home and his Dad had spoken to my Mum.

"Seems a nice man," said Mum. "We are going to drop you off at their house and then he will take you. We'll come on later to watch you and then if George's dad has had to leave, we can give him a lift home."

"Where exactly does he live?" I asked, realising it was strange that I had never known George's address. He certainly never had anyone back to his place after school.

"Oh, it's a very smart address," said Mum. "It's in one of those private roads behind the golf course."

That's why we found ourselves at three o'clock driving down Bryants Avenue, looking for The Maples. The houses were huge, with long drives and tucked away behind beautiful gardens with towering trees and electronic gates.

"It must be this one," I said. "It's the third driveway. Do you think we push this button?"

Mum had not managed to pull up within a hundred miles of the electronic key pad so I had to get out, run round, push the bell and then leap back into the car so we could drive through before the automatic gates shut on us. We got the giggles.

Mum spluttered through her laughter. "What if I can't ever escape again? I'll have to live in their summerhouse like a tramp and hope I'm not discovered! Come to think of it, I don't think I'd mind living in their summerhouse!"

She wasn't joking. There was a beautiful summerhouse, overlooking a pond, in front of the large modern house. A gardener was crouched in a flowerbed, weeding and the lawns looked like the centre court at Wimbledon. On day one!

The car crunched on the gravel as we pulled up outside the front door. We got out and stood awkwardly, like people who have arrived too early at a party and are not quite sure what to do. Just then, a man appeared round the side of the house. He was unmistakeably George's father, he had the same unusual sharply chiselled features and fair floppy hair. He reached out his hand.

"Hello! You must be Ellie – and Mrs Long. Do come in."

"Oh, I really must get on......" said mum, rather feebly. I grinned to myself. It wasn't often that you saw her lost for words!

We followed him through the front door and into a drawing room with a white carpet and a huge bunch of lilies on top of a highly polished grand piano. Only a glimpse of a wheelchair at the bottom of the wide staircase hinted of anything different about George's family. Only that and...I find it hard to explain what else, but there was a sort of emptiness, a sort of sadness in the house. George's dad was chatting away to mum, but he looked tired, stressed and nervously fiddled with his car keys all the time they were talking. The furniture was antique, the television in the next room was huge, the pool in the back garden looked inviting – but it felt almost like a stage set when the laughter had finished and the curtain had fallen.

George came in the room behind me and I jumped. He looked very ill at ease and anxious for us to get going. And it wasn't just the nerves about the performance.

"Let's go then Dad," he said.

His father asked him if he had said goodbye to his mother. George nodded and then his father added as explanation:

"George's mother doesn't go out much now, I'm afraid. She coped well after we had Tim – he's our second son who goes to Stoke Park – but then after losing the baby, she has been very depressed. It's not easy. Not easy for George, I mean. I have to be away a lot."

George had already left the room and was out on the drive. Mum said how sorry she was and if there was anything she could do......but George's dad seemed to be looking out of the window, as if by staring hard enough at the idyllic garden he owned, he could dream up another life where his children were well and his wife was happy.

You can have all the things in the world, I thought to myself, and yet have nothing. And, in a way, I suppose you can have very little and yet have everything. I knew more than most people how you could never put a price on a family. It didn't have to be a mum and a dad and a brother or sister. Not a family in that sense. But a family as in a group of people who love each other, laugh and cry together and are there for each other no matter what. Being here explained a lot about George. About his loneliness, his strangeness, his peculiarly grown up way of dealing with things. I think he probably was the grown up in this house, caring for his mum and his brother whilst his dad went away to escape the sadness.

I followed the parents outside, whilst Mr B set the burglar alarm and joined George who was waiting by the car.

"Dead posh pool!" I joked. "Trust you to only ask me here the day the heatwave finishes!"

And we laughed, which is often the best way of being friends and getting over awkwardness. We climbed in the back of the huge, spotless car and then George's dad got in the passenger seat. Which was odd to say the least. But the riddle was solved when the man we had seen putting the ladder away came and got in the driver's seat.

"All set sir?" he asked.

"All set, thank you Neville," he replied and with a purr of the engine, we pulled out of the drive and set off for Hampton. My eyes were out on stalks, but with a sad smile, George's dad turned round and looked me straight in the face.

"It's not as great as it looks, Ellie. George sticks up for me so he has probably not told you. I lost my licence for drink driving last year."

The George jigsaw was beginning to fit together: the bicycle, the comments about his dad and drugs, the fact he could not bring any cakes to the bake sale.....how much the band meant to him.

How much it meant to all of us, for different reasons. We had to win!

Chapter Thirteen: Winners and Losers

The venue was huge, the programme was glossy, the sound and lighting systems were totally professional and we were terrified! We managed to find the others in a big hall where all the various groups were gathered. We dumped our bags with our performance clothes and tried to look cool whilst we summed up the opposition. They all looked as though they already had recording contracts and were releasing their second album! I suppose looking back on it, that was rubbish and they were probably thinking the same about us, but that didn't make it any more reassuring at the time.

Shareen asked a tall boy with the group who were chatting next to us if he knew where we could find a run through schedule and he more or less ignored her. We could see Nicki and Toni and Dave and their band, Looking Black, flicking through the programme on the other side of the hall.

"I'm certainly not going to ask them for any help," said Shareen.

I was dying to go to the loo. George had gone into introvert mode. Adrian was tapping, as he always does when he's nervous and Liam was crushing a coke can in his one remaining functioning hand as though he was the bionic man.

"Look at us, man!" said Steve.

Liam laughed. "You didn't know you were joining Losers United when you agreed to play with us lot, did you?"

"Well, you weren't like this in Adrian's garage," agreed Steve. "What's got into you? You wouldn't be here if you hadn't blown the judges away at the school round. I heard you and you were incredible – and that was before I joined you! Just kidding-" he added quickly as Shareen went to slap him round the face!

163

"Seriously though," said Steve, "we have to believe in we right from the word go. And that means now. I'm going to get a rehearsal schedule and from then on its business. Agreed?"

"Agreed!" we all said, probably a little more convincingly than we felt inside.

When Steve got back with the schedule we saw that we only had to wait about half an hour before it was our turn for a run through. Ms Hensome appeared looking almost more nervous than us, we had equipment to shift, warm ups to do for the vocals in a small practice room and time flew. The run through went well. It was organised so no other groups could watch, which was reassuring because it meant we didn't all get freaked out by how good – or bad – everyone else was. We had some problem with feedback on the microphones, I missed the dreaded high note first time round and the lead kept coming out of the amplifier, but nothing unusual that we hadn't coped with before.

"OK, Glass Darkly, time's up. Great run through. Looking forward to the real thing!" said the sound technician enthusiastically, which was kind of him. We left the stage, taking a last glimpse at the echoing, empty auditorium. The next time we stood right there, it would be for real.

Now I've had a little rant about waiting before, so I won't go on. But this was waiting with a vengeance. People talk about killing time, but this was time killing me. We tried to have something to eat, but we all felt quite green. My stomach lurched like a bottomless pond and my breathing shuddered like a broken engine. It could stop at any moment, without warning and I would keel over and never be seen again. Everyone gets nervous in a different way, don't they? George got quieter and quieter until we wondered if he was still alive. Adrian – well you can guess what he did – he tapped. He was clinging on to his drumsticks as though his

164

life depended on them. He wasn't going to let Looking Black "lose" them for him this time. Shareen giggled most of the time, with an occasional burst of hysterical laughter at nothing much in particular and Liam paced up and down like a tiger in a zoo. Steve chewed gum. We must have been a right sight!

The atmosphere backstage in the hall was electrifying. Groups were called and we watched them follow the technician leading them to the green room. They may have had different clothes, with different images and different instruments, but they had two things in common: a burning desire to make music and a life-threatening attack of the nerves! A couple of minutes later, we would hear them through the speakers and another group would return to the hall, gasping with excitement and reliving every good note and every bad as they recovered from performing. And we were waiting.

We watched while Looking Black got their five minute call and then their final call. They looked good, all dressed in black, as they went up to the backstage area. Shareen even called out "Good Luck!" and they looked shocked. Nicki half turned round and called back "And you guys". She was like that. The only one of them who seemed to have a chink of kindness.

We could hear them on stage through the speakers and it was good. Other groups in the room were all commenting on how skilled the guitar work sounded. The applause from the audience was loud and long and I felt my heart sink a bit. I was sure we could never be as good as that. The last thing I could bear was for Looking Black to beat us, after all the evil things they had done.

The group two before us was incredible. Their lead singer had the classiest, bluesy type jazz voice you have ever heard. It made your flesh tingle and the strong, soulful songs reached deep into your heart and made you feel warm and sad at the same time. They were true talent and even everyone in the waiting hall burst into a round of applause when they finished their last number. We didn't see them come back in, because we were called up backstage to wait our go.

"Breathing. Concentrate on your breathing," Shareen whispered to me and I stood in the wings, my chest going in and out like a half inflated paddling pool! The reggae group before us were fun, but sounded like they needed a bit more rehearsal time and as they came off, they grinned and waved at us.

"Enjoy it, man!" said one boy, high fiving Adrian. "It's a real experience out there!"

"Wicked!" grinned their drummer.

"Awesome!"

And they were right. I tell you, walking out under those lights to a roar of applause ….we became performers. Or, to put it another way, our performance was bigger than us. We weren't just a little group of kids with problems and hang ups and worries about the size of our bums or the levels in our exams, we were musicians! And George was no longer the little weird kid from 7H: he was electrifying on the keyboard and as we got to the last chord, he punched the air and the audience went wild.

Walking back to the waiting room was a blur. A couple of stage hands and backstage crew slapped us on the back, saying things like "fantastic" and "I'll be wanting your autograph soon" – well that was to Steve and Shareen, not me, but I was part of it, all the same! We hugged each other and went over every chord, every note, every moment, just wanting to relive it.

"I want to go back on stage. I want to do it all again," said Adrian.

"Well, you may get a chance if you're in the last two," said Ms Hensome who had appeared with drinks and chocolate. We were suddenly all starving! "The best two have to do their third number, remember."

"And if we're in the last two, whatever happens, we either get a day in a recording studio and through to the nationals or we win £500 worth of tokens you can spend in music shops or on instruments or recording or whatever we want as a band..." Liam reminded us.

"I've been thinking." Shareen suddenly sounded quieter and more serious. "Thinking about what would happen if we won that £500."

"Spend it on beer!" joked Steve.

"No, seriously. I know it's a huge amount of money and all that. But I just wanted to suggest something. It doesn't matter if you don't agree. It's just a thought I had."

"Get on with it!" urged Liam. "It's like listening to the Head trying to talk about sex in assembly!"

"OK. Here goes!" said Shareen, with determination in her voice. "I think we're pretty good without spending £500 on equipment or lessons or instruments. We've got this far just as we are. We don't totally need that money. We can get by without it. So I was going to suggest that IF we won it, we could auction it off or cash it in or something and give the money to the Stoke Park Riding thing that Ellie and George have been doing the bake sales for. Then they would have £1000 by the end of term."

We all stared and although it must have been really noisy in the hall, it seemed as though it was totally silent and there was no-one there but us. George was doing what he always does when he's embarrassed, looking at the floor. I felt I couldn't really say anything. Part of me thought Shareen's idea was fantastic, but let's be honest, part of me also thought that it would be great to be able to make some recordings, or

167

buy a new guitar. It felt as though it was really up to Steve, Adrian and Liam. Steve led the way.

"I'll be honest," he said. "Its been amazing for me just to play with the group and have a chance to be here at the Regionals, so I don't feel I should have a say on what happens to the prizes. That's up to you guys and whatever you decide, is fine by me."

Shareen looked at Liam and Adrian. Liam grinned.

"I'm sort of the other way round from Steve. I never thought I'd be here once I broke my finger, so in a way I've been lucky once already. Who needs two lots of luck? If we win the £500, I'm cool with the idea of giving it to the little kids."

So it was Adrian left. He looked up, sideways, caught my eye and turned to stare out of the long hall window at the pale evening sky. Money was tight in their house. There weren't too many treats. Adrian had been saying for ages how much he needed a new bass drum and how a decent one cost about two hundred quid. I didn't want this to split the band, so I spoke before he had a chance.

"This is really hard for Adrian. You and me Shareen, we don't need anything really, just to sing. And Liam's just got a new guitar. And George..." I was going to say something about George's family been really rich and being able to afford whatever they wanted, but thank goodness I stopped myself just in time. "But Adrian," I carried on, "Adrian really needs a new bass drum and this is probably the only way he's going to get it. If everyone agrees, why don't we split it? Give £250 to the charity and some to Adrian for the drum kit?"

"Hey forget it!" said Adrian. "If we're good enough to win £500 worth of tokens and come second in the regional finals with my old set, then why do I need a new one? No, I agree with Shareen. If we win, let's give it to the charity. But one small thing…."

"Yes?" asked Shareen, halfway hugging Adrian and Steve.

"We haven't won yet!"

"And another thing" added Liam.

"Yes?" the rest of us all said together, laughing.

"We're probably going to come first and win the recording studio deal and the trip to the nationals and then we'll be so famous we'll be able to build our very own riding stables!"

All our joking stopped very quickly though, because the announcer was asking all the band members to make their way to the stage for the judges announcements. This was it. We stood on stage whilst the audience gave all of us – all ten bands – a standing ovation! Get on with it, I was thinking, forget the clapping. Miles Unal, the guitarist for Mobsters Inc. (and if you haven't heard of him, you're prehistoric) came out to announce the judges' decision. They said they had three Highly Commended to announce first, then they would give the names of the two bands who were to play again to see who would go through to the finals. So, in those circumstances, part of you wants to be Highly Commended because at least it means you got somewhere and they thought you had talent. But the other part of you doesn't want to hear your name, because that means you can't possibly be one of the winners.

"And the Highly Commended Bands are:
Rock Solid from Metherton High, particularly for their fantastic harmony work, The Mandarins from Haywards School for the Performing Arts – Guys, we really loved the instrumental sections - and finally, from Canterton Combined College…."

Time froze! We looked at each other and then across the stage at Nicki and Dave and the rest of their band. All of us

169

in the same boat. We wanted to be called and we didn't want to be called...

"Looking Black!"

We clapped and watched them hugging each other, Nicki with tears in her eyes as she went up to shake hands with Miles Unal. It wasn't clear if they were tears of happiness or disappointment. We still had all the waiting to come.

"So, on to the last two bands. And before I announce the names......"

Was he never going to finish? Did he know how much agony we were all in?

"I would like to say that the standard this year has been incredible and that both these bands deserve to go on to the Nationals. It's just a shame that only one can go. But that's the rules, so the two bands the judges would like to hear play again are Glass Darkly..."

At that point, I think I must have almost passed out. Liam was as white as a sheet and before we knew it we were being hustled off stage ready for the play offs. I hadn't even heard who we were up against.

"It's Southern Tracks, you know the one with the fantastic black girl as their lead vocalist," said Shareen.

"Just like us!" said Steve.

They were good. There was no doubt about it, they were an amazing band. We were going to have to pull out all the stops and perform like we had never performed before if we were in with a chance. This time we listened on our own in the vast, empty hall. All the other bands and performers were in the auditorium listening to the finalists. We sat on blue plastic chairs, surrounded by empty drink cans, discarded hoodies, electric guitars and half eaten packets of jaffa cakes and listened to Southern Tracks reach notes you only half dreamed existed and awaken memories you had forgotten you had.

"Wow" said George. "I don't mind being beaten by them."

"We're not going to be beaten by anyone!" I said. "We're going to London."

And with that, we went back on stage for the last time to sing "No More Ghosts". And all our ghosts were put to rest for those three minutes. Ghosts of lost mothers and dead mothers and depressed mothers; ghosts of lost homelands in Africa or private sadnesses we hadn't even shared with each other. We were all strong creators and on that stage, we believed in ourselves. "No More Ghosts" we sang, repeating the last line, getting quieter and quieter until Shareen's final solo notes. "No More Ghosts". For a split second there was complete silence. The audience were captivated. Then they erupted. As the lights went down and curtain fell, we all had tears in our eyes. Win or lose, the performance was ended and there is always left inside you a mixture of high and low, the ecstasy of performing and the emptiness of finishing.

The judges brought us back on stage: Southern Tracks on one side of the stage and us, Glass Darkly, on the other. Miles Unal came back up, but this time with the Head of the Recording Studio donating the first prize and the chairman of the company which financed the £500 vouchers for the second prize. He was in a suit and looked a bit uncomfortable in the spotlight, surrounded by pop stars and teenagers! They all said their bit about how wonderful everything and everyone was and we are all just thinking, get on with it, get on with it, get on with it and then we heard the words.....

"But there has to be a winner. So I would like to announce that the judges' decision has been unanimous and representing this region in the National Bands Final for this year will be ......Southern Tracks!"

What is it about coming second? It's a fantastic achievement, as everyone will tell you for the next week, but – let's face it – it's not first. And first was what we had come for. You can say you don't mind, but you do. At least I do. It's like when Bridie comes second in one of her athletic races, I always say, but that's incredible. You ran such a fast time. That means you're the second best in the area at the 100m. But she always looks at me and says "I didn't enter the race to come second. I wanted to win."

So we shook hands, looked pleased, congratulated the others, went through the motions. But when it came down to it, we were second. We weren't going to London.

The judges were asking Shareen to come forward to accept the vouchers on behalf of the band and everyone was clapping and then I noticed that she asked if she could say a few words. Then I remembered. Surely she wasn't brave enough to do that now?

Shareen coughed and started speaking into the microphone, slowly and a bit unsure of herself to start with, but then with more confidence.

"We wanted to say thank you to We R Music for sponsoring this competition and for the £500 vouchers. But we also wanted to say that we would like to either auction off this prize or exchange it for money, to give to an appeal we have been supporting. Ellie and George, our vocalist and keyboard player, have been raising money to buy specialist equipment to allow local disabled children to go riding. With another £500 they will have reached their target of £1000 and we think that is the best use of our prize." Then she looked a bit worried.

"If that's OK with you," she added.

The audience were all clapping, but I could see the chairman of We R Music talking to Miles Unal and some other officials up on the stage. There was a bit of a pause, and then the man in the suit took the microphone from Shareen and tapped it twice. He began to speak.

"Ladies and Gentleman. I am sure you agree with me that it is fantastic to see a group of young people who are not only so talented, but also prepared to give so much to help other children not so fortunate as themselves. I think you made an incredible offer, Glass Darkly, but I am not going to allow you to exchange the vouchers, or auction them off…"

I looked at George and Adrian. I couldn't see the others' faces in the lights, but I guessed they must be thinking the same as me. We hadn't expected him to say no!

"No! What I am going to do is present you with the vouchers, with great pleasure, and make a donation from WRM, to your charity of £500 as well."

Adrian flung his arms around me. We were all amazed, but it probably meant more to him than any of us! Everyone in the auditorium was on their feet cheering and the man in the suit went quite pink! They presented the prizes to Southern Tracks and their gorgeous lead singer couldn't really say anything because she was crying. She was so beautiful that I am sure if she doesn't make it as a singer, she could be a model and then Southern Tracks played their last song all over again as an encore.

We sang our own encore going home in the car, "No More Ghosts", which was probably more true than they knew. If I could keep my promise to the Green Lady and bring the children back to Highwood, maybe she and her baby would be at peace and there would be no more ghosts and they at least would be winners.

Chapter Fourteen: Coming Home

Where is she now, I wondered. Is she watching? The silence seemed deep and strong, although I was aware of noises away in the distance. Children shouting, an airplane high in the blue summer sky, a car door slamming. The strong sunlight seemed to shimmer over the roses and create a haze in the little secret garden. Nothing was solid; everything seemed to shift, and it was as if the air was full of incense like a church. I read once that the Buddhists tie their prayers to flags so that the wind can carry their prayers to heaven. Perhaps this summer breeze can carry my prayers too.

I had come back to Highwood. Come back with George and Bridie and Javaad, and this time with all the members of Glass Darkly to present the cheque for the new riding equipment. Josh and the staff at Stoke Park had arranged quite an occasion. The chairman of the record company was coming with some people from his office. Lots of kids from Stoke were going to be there, including George's brother Tim, who I had never met. I'd never been back to his house, in fact and we had never really spoken of that one, sad visit ever again. Obviously all the riding staff from Highwood were going to be there and the presentation was going to take place at the stables. The local press had been alerted and were turning up. Someone even said there might be a TV crew.

I had managed to slip away from everybody for a few minutes and come down to the garden. I wanted time to be by myself and to think about everything that had happened in the past few weeks. It seemed as though everything had worked out in the end. OK, we had not won the band competition, but we had achieved more than we had ever dreamt was possible and – in a sense – we were winners in the way it turned out, because it helped us raise the £1000 for the riding. And I was sure that The Green Lady would rest peacefully again, once she knew that the children with disabilities, children like her own poor baby, born unwanted and unloved all those years ago and buried unchristened and unacknowledged in this very garden – that once she knew the children would be back, then she could be at peace. Would I see her again? Part of me really wanted to, because I was beginning to wonder how much I had seen and how much I had imagined. But then I remembered little Alice and sitting with Josh and that teacher and George in the locked room, hearing the sad story of the Bickleys. It had happened. It had been real. Part of me feared seeing her again.

Being over at the stables, saying hello to Jo and the teachers and getting ready for the presentation had reminded me about the ponies at Mr Wiltons's farm. That was the only part of the summer which had not worked out. It was true, the ponies were not there any longer. I had walked that way twice now, once on my own and once with Bridie and there was no sign of them. I had even tried to take a new route through the farm fields to see if he had put them somewhere else, but nothing. No tell tale hoof prints, no headcollars on the gate, nothing. I was sad, but I had to tell myself that he had probably sold them to the slaughterhouse.

I had summoned the courage to try to talk to Nicki about it at school. She had been on her own in the canteen and when it was just the two of us, we usually got on. She had even come up to us and congratulated us on coming second in the competition. Dave had been with her and he said he'd been really impressed with the drumming. So perhaps they weren't so bad after all. It was just their vile younger sister Toni who went on and on becoming more and more unpleasant. The only good thing was that she had bullied so many people in our year group now that she was fast running out of people who were willing to hang around with her. I think that was why she was spending more and more time bunking off school. I wonder how she felt when she didn't bother to come in. Same as me? Probably not, as she had a whole group of friends at other schools who never bothered to go. No old pervert would proposition them in the park: they looked too scary.

Anyway, I had gone up to Nicki and said:

"Nicki. I'm not trying to be nosey or anything, but I just wondered if your cousin knew what had happened to the two ponies on Mr Wilton's farm. It's just that they're not there any longer...."

Nicki looked at me a bit suspiciously. Although she was Year 9, I know people said she wasn't very clever and that was maybe why she tried to act big sometimes. She obviously decided it was safe to talk.

"I don't really know. You might think Fraser is horrible, but d'you know, he really loves animals. One of the reasons he got the job on the farm was because he wants to work with animals, but they only give him the machinery because that's what he's good at. He wouldn't hurt animals if he could help it."

I was a bit doubtful about this Fraser turned St. Francis story. It certainly hadn't looked that way when I saw him.

"Well, if that's the case, how come he didn't say anything to Mr Wilton then about the way he was keeping the ponies?"

Nicki took another crisp out of her bag and ate it slowly.

"You don't really understand, do you?" she said. "I'm not being mean or anything but your family, you're all quite well off and doing OK, aren't you?"

"What's that got to do with anything?" I replied, a bit angrily but then I saw that Nicky might get up and move if I continued, so I backed down. "I mean, yes, you're probably right. We are quite lucky, but I don't understand where that fits in."

Nicky stared at me. "It's like this. Fraser is on an ASBO. He got in lots of trouble but really wants to turn things around now. He doesn't do drugs now, or drink so much, so it's really important to him to have found a job. It may not be much and it may not pay much and it might not be exactly what he wants to do. But it is a job and it's helping him stay out of trouble and out of prison. What would happen if he started to go on to his boss about the way he kept the animals? "

"I suppose he'd get the sack," I said slowly.

"Yeah. Then he'd be right back at square one. The ponies would still be dying, but he would be worse off as well. So it isn't as easy as you think."

She was right. I did sometimes rush in and see things in black and white. Life often was a lot more complicated than it appeared. Like George for instance. There wasn't much else I could say, so I left Nicky there in the canteen. If the ponies were dead, well, maybe that was the end of their suffering and although it wasn't fair, perhaps it was the best thing for them. When I thought of some man turning up with a gun and then dragging their little bodies out to a trailer and off to a factory, I had tears in my eyes. I was sure they would have known. Horses are sensitive like that. But it would have been over very quickly.

I picked a daisy from the lawn and then another one. I made a tiny slit in the stalk of the first daisy and threaded them together. A daisy chain. Like life. How it all fits together. And when I had made a little bracelet, I stood up and left the garden. I thought I could take it home and press it and put it in my special box, with all the other odds and ends which made up the special memories of my jigsaw life.

I looked at my watch. It was nearly twelve o'clock and everyone would be gathering at the stables.

"There's Ellie!" I heard Bridie call. And she waved, beckoning me over. So many people had arrived since I slipped away. There must have been about a hundred people there. About eight of the children from Stoke Park were mounted on the ponies, beaming from ear to ear.

"That's Tim," said George to me, pointing to a smiling boy on a lovely dun pony.

"Who's that with him?" I asked, pointing to the woman holding the bridle and chatting to Tim.

"That's my mum!" said George.

"Your mother's here?" I looked astonished. "I thought, I mean, but without being rude or anything, your dad said she never really went out any more."

"Well, after dad told her all about our band evening, she realised how much she was missing. So she went to some special doctor who apparently your mum recommended and said she wanted some help, that she wanted to get out and about. Tim was so thrilled she was coming today."

"Was it hard for her?" I asked.

George nodded. "I think so. At one point I thought she wasn't going to make it. But dad helped her and here she is. Hopefully it's the first big step. She looks happy doesn't she?"

I smiled. "And so do you," I said. He acknowledged that with a nod. Nothing more. But George and I don't need to use too many words to understand each other.

Apparently it was my job to make a speech. Mum had helped me write it and I had made some notes on a piece of paper, but now that it was time, I couldn't find it. I suddenly realised I had left it in the pocket of my jacket, which was in the car. In the car park. Miles away from the stables. My tongue felt huge and my mind went totally blank.

I heard Josh saying "And now I think Ellie has something she wants to present."

I did not have a choice. At least I hadn't left the cheque in the car. That would have been a disaster. I walked up to the railings and started to speak. Somehow the words just came.

"This isn't really from me, but from loads and loads of people who helped to raise the money for the special equipment here so that the children from Stoke Park can still come riding. And especially from We R Music who gave us loads of money.

It's difficult to explain how this whole thing started, but when we signed up to come here for our activity week, the brochure promised us we would experience a different world. And we certainly did." I caught Josh's eye at that point and he smiled. Only a few of us knew how different. "We saw how special this place is, how it was left by the Bickley family so that all kids, and especially kids with disabilities could learn and have fun and do outdoors things. And that was the first time I ever tried riding. Actually I tried lots of things for the first time, but as I spent the whole sailing lesson three feet underwater, I think riding was a bit more successful!" Everyone laughed then, which was good because it felt less formal. I was becoming more confident.

"Jo and everyone here were so good at making me feel confident, so I knew how it must feel for Stoke Park to come here every week and how awful it must feel to be losing that. So when we heard that the riding was going to have to finish, a few of us decided to try to raise the money and – here we are."

And with that, in a rather feeble way I handed over the cheque. I wasn't actually sure who to give it to. Whether it should be Josh, on behalf of Highwood, or Jo, as the leader of the riding, or the teachers from Stoke Park. In the end they

180

all held a bit of it while the cameras flashed and the children cheered.

I turned away, but Jo stopped me.

"Before you go, Ellie, I have a surprise for you."

I couldn't think what she was talking about. George and Javaad and Bridie were giggling like they already knew something, and my parents looked suspicious as well.

"What do you mean?" I asked. I don't really like surprises. Most of the surprises I've had in my life have been unpleasant and so I am understandably a bit wary.

"Bring them on, please Fraser!" called Jo, looking to the big barn behind the stables.

At first I couldn't understand what was happening. A man was leading a couple of ponies towards the crowd. They looked very jumpy, faced with all those people, but he held their headcollars firmly. Then I looked a bit closer. The man looked familiar. He looked a bit like Nicky. He looked like, in fact he was, Fraser. Her cousin. From the farm. Except that he was smiling and patting the horses, not snarling and shouting.

"Do you recognise these two?" Jo asked me.

I walked slowly over to the ponies, which put their ears forward and shied away a bit.

"Careful, they're still a bit nervous" said Jo.

As I got closer I could see a scar behind the ear of the little grey, the pony nearest me. But that was about the only way I could recognise the ponies, my ponies from the farm. Here they were, with shining coats and bright eyes, lively and interested in their surroundings. Happy! They weren't dead after all. They weren't shot and sent to some factory. Nor were they hidden away in some other awful paddock. They were here, safe, at Highwood!

"How on earth....?" I was lost for words. I looked round at the laughing faces around me for an explanation.

"I think Fraser can tell you" said Josh.

Fraser told me how he had wanted to save the ponies but didn't know how. Then he had heard from Nicky about the cake sale at school and how that was for the riding for the disabled at Highwood. Mr Wilton had been talking about having the ponies put down because they were nothing but trouble now the Horse Rescue Centre were on to them and Fraser needed to find an alternative – fast. So he had a brainwave. He had rung Highwood and spoken to Jo. Told her about the ponies, about how nice their characters were and about how they just needed feeding up and looking after and how brilliant they would be for the riding school. And the rest was easy to work out. Jo had come over with the horsebox and Mr Wilton had been glad to see the back of them.

"So Brownie and Fudge are now part of our stables" said Jo "named after your bake sale! And Fraser is part of the stables too. He is working here part time now, as a stable hand."

When all the clapping and talking had died down, Josh told everyone that there were drinks and eats over in the main house and so we all started to make our way over there. Mum was busy chatting with loads of people who she knew from Stoke Park. Bridie and her mum were talking with George and his family and Javaad had gone off with Lewis for a secret and illegal go on the ropes course!

After I'd grabbed an orange juice and a handful of twiglets, I left the main hall and went upstairs. I checked down the staircase to see if anyone was looking, then quickly tried the handle to the locked room. I had the sense that it was locked and open at the same time. Opening for me. I pushed the door and slipped inside the room and closed the door behind me.

Epilogue

Nothing had changed. The air still smelled of lavender, the sheets on the bed were clean and crisp, there were fresh roses in the vase on the table. I sat on the little nursing chair and looked out of the window. The room felt peaceful. Quiet. A lot of the summer had been about putting things right, making things happen. The term was almost over now and next year we would all be in Year 8. There were lots of things I didn't know. Would the band stay together? Would we, as friends, stay together? Nothing would ever separate me and Bridie, that much was certain! Would Adrian's dad marry Jenny? Would George's mum start to recover? Would all the small hopeful seeds which had been planted, continue to grow? And could I even bear to think about life continuing to be so good, so happy? Because to believe in that is a risk.

One thing was clear to me. As clear as the pure water in the sparkling fountain. I felt stronger. Inside. I had managed to move up to secondary school, despite all my worries. I had spent another year with my new family. In my dreams last night, the children had returned, playing in that alley, laughing as they ran between the broken bottles and the scuttling crisp packets. Then it had seemed as if the little girl in the wheelchair turned and smiled – at me. The others stopped their game and also waved before they melted away through walls and fences like mist over the sea on an autumn evening.

I nodded as I remembered. Farewell. I like to think I had, in the end, been able to give them what they sought. They were at peace. I took one last look around the room and stood up. As I turned away from the window, my eye caught the ornate gold mirror on the facing wall. I saw in the glass the reflection of a lady who was not in the room. She was looking down at a baby in her arms and smiling. Her long dark hair was loose and fell over her face. For one brief, timeless moment, she looked up and our eyes met. Then the Green Lady was gone.

Now we see through a glass darkly, then we will see face to face.

Lightning Source UK Ltd.
Milton Keynes UK
25 November 2009

146710UK00002B/18/P